CW00729738

Annie Mu

John Murray was born in West Cumbria in 1950. He read Sanskrit at Oxford and for a time did research into Classical Indian medicine. He founded the acclaimed short story magazine *Panurge* which flourished between 1984 and 1996 and was widely recognised as Britain's premier fiction journal. His novels are *Samarkand* (1985), *Kin,* (1986), *Radio Activity* (1993) and *Reiver Blues* (1996). In 1988 he won the prestigious Dylan Thomas Award. He is married with one daughter and lives in Brampton, Cumbria, in the far north-east of the county.

by the same author

SAMARKAND (Aidan Ellis)
KIN (Aidan Ellis)
RADIO ACTIVITY (Sunk Island)
REIVER BLUES (Flambard)

PLEASURE

John Murray

PANURGE
PUBLISHING

1996

PLEASURE by JOHN MURRAY

first published by Aidan Ellis 1987
first Panurge Publishing edition 1996

PRODUCTION Henry Swan
COVER Colin Brownson

Typeset at Union Lane Telecentre, Brampton, Cumbria CA8 1BX
Tel. 016977-41014

Printed by Peterson Printers, 12 Laygate, South Shields
Tyne and Wear NE33 5RP
Tel. 0191-456-3493

ISBN 1 898984 35 2

British Library Cataloguing in Publication Data.
A catalogue record for this book is available from
the British Library.

PANURGE PUBLISHING
Crooked Holme Farm Cottage,
Brampton,
Cumbria CA8 2AT
Tel. 016977-41087

*for my wife Annie
and in memory of Bill*

Natural Learning and *The Señor and the Celtic Cross* first appeared in the London Review of Books.

Those Who Scorn Sir Walter Scott and *Not At All!* first appeared in London Magazine.

A Ticket To Bombay first appeared in Fiction Magazine.

Master of Ceremonies first appeared in Stand Magazine.

The Señor and the Celtic Cross also appeared in New Stories 8 and *Master of Ceremonies* in Best Short Stories 1986.

PLEASURE

Natural Learning

Logan stood outside the shop which looked like an English funeral parlour, black-painted and all its contents invisible. On the window was inscribed in English in impressive calligraphy LEGAL OPIUM AND GANJA SHOP FOR HOLY MEN. It lay along one of those relatively deserted back streets of central Calcutta, the only wayfarers being the trams and the cadaverous dogs who roamed like wolves in their desperate packs.

This city was certainly an assault on his European nervous system, one both hypnotic and unreal. One minute he was struck by something, some sight or some person colourfully exaggerated, the next by a starkness of miserable humanity so stark, so very miserable, it refused at all to sink in. It stayed on as some bizarre cartoon impression, some graphic, thoroughly unreal stroke of impersonal, affectless design. It so happened that the sight of starvation - especially in-children - made Logan crave absurd palliatives like sweets, ice-creams and cakes for himself. He was for ever stopping at those little cigarette stalls to purchase half a dozen boiled sweets, all of which he would swallow within five minutes or so...

The streets were black and dingy, factories or warehouses they seemed to be composed of, though there was no noise of industry nor population. It was a problem what exactly constituted these streets where only cur packs and speeding trams would roam. Almost as problematic as the errand Logan was engaged in; to wit, to find himself a primer on Bengali. He had got it into his head that he wanted to learn the language of Calcutta and someone somewhere on his travels had recommended a particular text, *Sahaj Path,* used by Bengalis themselves to teach their infant children. Logan wanted that particular primer and no other. Yet that primer was not to be had. He had been to about six bookshops already and on his way had picked up plenty of second-hand novels in English; *Lolita; The Genius and the Goddess* (an Indian reprint of the

1

English pundit who had written so sympathetically of matters Indian...); a fiction by Koestler about a man who had psychologically lost the use of his legs... plenty of Western literature in fact, but no sign at all of *Sahaj Path.*

He decided to return the way he'd come and was just about to take a right turning for a central and spacious avenue, when he bumped headlong into a hustler.

The startled hustler held some thin, colourful necklaces in his hands. He was short, skinny, about twenty-five (meaning middle-aged by street standards), thinly-moustached and almost good-looking. His eyes lit up when they beheld the shy and hungry-looking Logan. At once he seemed to sense Englishness, youth, lack of firm direction, interest in the more selfish personal satisfactions.

'Sahib, you like some jewels, sir?'

He waved the absurd necklaces before Logan's eyes. They were garish, tawdry baubles, worth nothing as far as an amateur like Logan could guess. Why on earth would Logan be supposed to want those pathetic, pitiable things?

He shook his head politely and moved on. The hustler moved swiftly backwards and improvised other possibilities.

'Cigarettes? Very cheap cigarettes? Hashish? Hashish that is not too costly?'

Logan again shook his head and kept on walking. The little man, however, would not give way.

'Opium? Heroin? Heroin that is not over-costly?'

Logan made no reply. But he was beginning to feel greatly irritated.

'A woman? You would like a lady, a young, curvy lady, a very young lady, or a very old madam perhaps for sahib?'

'Sh...' began Logan, giving the skinny little man a bit of a push.

'A man? A boy? A *little* boy? Who is not *very* costly?'

'Oh - bugger off!' shouted Logan fiercely.

That stopped the hustler. His face fell and he looked genuinely grieved. He pointed at Logan and said beseechingly:

'Sahib, that is no way to speak to me! That is no way to

speak to *anyone,* words like that!'

Logan grunted and hurried on. But the little man's words gradually sank in and he began to feel ashamed of himself. He felt shame that he was like every other young European dawdling and tramping around Indian cities. After a few weeks of the ceaseless begging, pestering, chasing by the poor-poor, the rich-poor, the starving hustlers, the cracked astrologers, the dealers in drugs, sex, jewellery, temple idols... everything short of cow dung itself... the young travellers all became rude, often self-indulgently scornful. They pushed beggars out of the way, like ancient feudal squires. All of them young and liberal, some politically radical, all compassionate under comfortable domestic circumstances, yet somehow the fierce heat and the sheer population encountered in large Indian cities... all this was enough to make them as peevish and tyrannical as the haughtiest in creation.

He passed a penniless family living on a scrap of mat on the pavement. That scrap of mat was their permanent address, a freehold property so to say. They didn't even bother to beg. They were all asleep, enjoying the poor man's, woman's, child's luxurious solace. They were lying outside a dairy, which sold fresh milk for saried middle-class housewives, as well as chocolate milk for special occasions. Logan hesitated over whether to leave some rupees on the mat. He hesitated so long he ended up feeling foolish, and then moved on away leaving nothing. Meanwhile he was looking for copies of his Bengali primer. Then he would be able to tell hustlers to go the devil in their own tongue. Turning to take a guilty look back at the family on its mat, he bumped into someone, a someone who seemed at that bump sharply to retract and mumble in a man's voice something strange. Logan turned to apologise...

But instead cried out...

Because the man's face was half eaten-away. It was like a maggotted cheese, exactly so. What should have been a face was like some crumbled Gorgonzola. Yet it was a man. It was a leper. Logan was flooded by the streams from his adrenals. He dived into his pockets and within two seconds had a five rupees dropped into the outstretched hand of the leper. The hand - he only flashed his eyes upon it - was a leper's hand, it wasn't one needing a half-hour manicure.

'Sahib,' whimpered the Gorgonzola.

'I'm sorry,' gasped Logan, speeding on for his *Sahaj Path,* almost wanting to weep as a matter of fact, though not specifically for the young leper...

He stopped several hundred yards on and tremblingly lit himself a *shiv biri,* a rolled tobacco leaf, costing one rupee for a fat pack of fifty. It was nearing lunchtime and he realised he was extraordinarily hungry. He wanted a fried lamb cutlet, potato chips, tomato sauce and an ice-cream for his sweet. And some coffee, some comforting European coffee. He looked about for a suitable restaurant. And just then, as his eyes alighted on one, a skinny little waif of a man approached him.

Logan groaned to himself and flinched. Every approach from every poor-looking Indian was by now a cause of flinching. Such an attitude was shameful - yet why should he disguise it? And yet... this one... this little man did not make Logan as distrustful as he might have. This was largely because the little man looked harassed, seemed worried, and because underneath that worry was a basic integrity of expression, something one might have called a simple honesty. He looked like he had a problem, like a hundred million or so other desperate Indians. And Logan, moreover, felt quite simply and unselfconsciously as if he was responsible for all of them, that it was he and his like who had caused all these problems. It was no reasoned political nor sociological analysis had led to this, it was no more than his naivest egotistical instincts.

'How are you?' began the runty little man in a capable English pronunciation. His face was thin, anxious and sincere, his eyes gentle, his body undernourished and feeble-looking. He spoke in a simple, brotherly way to the tourist. 'You seem to have some problem. Are you looking for something?'

Logan warily explained that he was searching for a restaurant. Eyeing up the little Indian the Englishman decided he must be some minor clerk, some small-time teacher or petty official in temporary distress. He was most likely in his middle to late thirties. The little man evidently had a cough, not a violent racking cough, but one persistent and slight. He wore a striped, dowdy-looking shirt and a pair of equally dowdy trousers. He looked both desperate and somehow available, someone stood there to help or otherwise engage a rather directionless European like Logan.

They conversed. The Indian whose name was George and who was a Christian immediately desired to help Logan in his search for the Bengali primer. The Englishman did not particularly desire any company, but on the other hand he hadn't the heart to refuse such an unselfish offer. Yet - he was still ravenously hungry. Therefore, he compromised by offering George some lunch in the nearby café.

'I'm afraid 1 haven't the money,' said George.

'No,' explained Logan gently. 'I'm asking you to lunch, Mr Gokhale.'

They entered the café, a striking-looking pair. Inside it was chock-full, but they managed to find themselves a little corner table. Some of the customers looked rather curiously, not to say intently, at the spectacle of George Gokhale. This was a café frequented by the better-off class of clerk and teacher, the lower-middle-class of Calcutta, those who daily cultivate a specialised taste for such European commonplaces as chipped potatoes and bottled tomato sauce....

Gokhale with great nervousness ordered a dish identical to Logan's. His body was bent towards the table, as if he had no right to be there. He looked pained. Logan on the other hand felt defiant and stared back at the other customers as aggressively as he could. Which was a waste of time. Staring has a different, unintelligible language in the East. Our psychologists of eye-contact would have all their graphs made skew in a Calcutta café.

'Where do you work, Mr Gokhale?' Logan asked him, rather irritated by the situation already. 'Are you... a teacher?'

Gokhale shook his head, a little wearily. He held a single chipped potato at wary arm's length. 'No. No, I am not a teacher. I earn only odds and ends, Mr Logan. Only bits and pieces, that is to say. I mean that I do casual jobs and live very poorly. Sometimes - last week - I had a job for so many days, but other times I have no job at all. Sometimes I have some clerical work with a carpet factory. Other times I just stand about because I have no work to do.'

Logan grew sympathetic. 'Like today?'

Gokhale nodded, with a grimace. At which Logan guiltily mumbled, 'And starve? You go without food?'

The Indian nodded again. He seemed patiently puzzled, stupefied by his misfortunes. He explained that his home was a square of mat upon a terrace, the balcony of a hotel belonging to a rapacious landlord who let him sleep there for an exorbitant sum. No, he was not married. For who would marry Gokhale with his prospects? And where would he live with his wife? In a dustbin he asked without self-pity? Still, he continued in mournful singsong manner, what consoled him was his faith, his devotion to Jesus, that gave him firm hope when all else was hopeless. Logan, attentive as he was, wasn't quite sure whether this dull little man was as convinced as his declaration tried to be. He thought he detected a slight unction in that devotion. Or he might have dreamt it. How would he ever know for certain?

'Are you a Christian?' asked Gokhale seriously. 'Of course you have to be, in one sense, as an Englishman...'

'Without faith,' answered Logan dryly. 'Just now I bumped into a leper with his face eaten away. I cried out and ran off. I gave him five rupees but I was scared of him. In fact I was terrified. A fine Christian I would make.'

George looked at him curiously. He said with concern that you could get disease from contact with such men. Logan hungrily finished off his meat cutlet and then asked: 'Is there no state support? I mean can you get no money from the government to stop you from starving?'

Gokhale scowled with patient puzzlement. 'Yes,' he answered, 'there is an office, a place in the city centre, where the destitute may queue for their Social Security. You might queue all day. And the next day. And the next day. And so on.

6

After you have waited there ten hours, the clerk will close the window in your face and tell you to come back the day after tomorrow. He wants to go for his tea. He should come back but no he decides not to come back. Also, he laughs very often in your face. The day after tomorrow of course you will not be in the front of the queue again. Then, if by a miracle you finally get your assistance, it is so very small...'

Logan frowned and felt painfully gloomy. Then, rebelliously, he ordered the pair of them enormous ice-creams, ones six inches high with cream, fruit and chocolate. The garish sweet plainly terrified George Gokhale, yet he waded his way bravely through it. As they sipped their coffees, Logan remarked of his sheepish coughing: 'Are you ill? What is it that makes you cough?'

Gokhale sucked his coffee hungrily. 'I think tuberculosis,' he replied uneasily. 'But I have no money to see the doctor yet. I don't know. It stops me doing manual work. With manual work I could eat some days. The days I cannot be a clerk, that is.'

Eventually Gokhale went into a whispering, fervent monologue about his Christian faith and about the love and kindness of his fellow devotees; all poor, all desperate, all struggling. At which Logan squirmed and felt greatly embarrassed. To him it seemed thin rubbish, in the face of no-face Gorgonzola and that child sleeping on a square of mat twelve months of every year. Meanwhile George was timidly pulling out a crumpled letter, one lovingly handled as if it had been a thousand-rupee note. Instead, it turned out to be a beautifully written letter from a girl in Esbjerg, a Danish Christian who had met up with Gokhale in Calcutta and had shared some street excursions and conversations with him. It was a devotional letter, a weird, syrupy letter that made Logan squirm as all evangelical matters did. There were no rough edges to such matters, no jagged contradictions. Helplessly he felt annoyed, even disgusted with George Gokhale. In his boat he would have hustled, stolen, cheated, done *something* sooner than starve and walk round with that hangdog all-enduring meekness. That at any event was what he thought as he

7

shovelled down the last of his sickly dessert.

After their meal George suggested they walk onto the central boulevard where all the biggest and finest shops abounded. There they would be sure to find some copies of *Sahaj Path*. And it was just outside the café that they passed a huddle of hard-looking, spiv-looking young men. They must, the tourist supposed, be shopowners, businessmen of some sort, all of them in their middle-twenties. They all looked fairly healthy and gazed fairly contemptuously at Gokhale. They muttered something in Bengali to George and George looked at them most discomfited. They made obscene gestures at their backsides. Logan scowled. He turned and gave them two fingers and a string of obscenities. They laughed, much amused. But Gokhale quickly took his arm and said to ignore them.

'I know them,' he said worriedly. 'They are corrupt. They are friendly with the police' - he pointed to a hotel, a dingy-looking facade nearby 'You see that place there? If ever you went to get a room there...'

'I did,' interrupted Logan. 'Last week I did. And it was full. Five times I went back.'

'It is no hotel,' the Indian answered dryly. 'It is a brothel. Run by those men. It is a brothel especially for the local police force. I do not offend such men or they would set the police on me, Mr Logan.'

The tourist shivered.

'The police of course can do what they like,' Gokhale continued glumly. 'To men and families who live on the street or on terraces of poor hotels. No one seems to notice, Mr Logan, if a few families on their mats just disappear...'

Logan, horrified, felt his blood blaze up.

'And how often does it happen? That someone just disappears?'

Gokhale shrugged pacifically. 'No one would know if it did or not. They have no friends. It is a large city. Full of immigrants without name or number. Do you not see the problem, Mr Logan?'

By now, they had arrived at the grand boulevard. It was

wide, broad, imperial, the gift of Logan's distant ancestors. On the other side was a park, on this side some of the most select of shops in Calcutta. At once they were assailed by about a dozen ragged shoe cleaners; men, boys and virtual babes. Gokhale gestured and shouted at them but Logan insisted that both of them should have their shoes cleaned. As they stood - the Indian shuffling embarrassedly, sheepishly - the seven-year-old shoe cleaner pointed dismissively to the eight cleaners who had been turned away.

'These fellows are all most ignorant,' he squeaked with a confident grin. 'They do not know English as brilliantly as I.'

Logan smiled and pulled the little boy's ear and gave him twenty rupees, an enormous sum. Gokhale frowningly chided him for giving so much. He led the Englishman into a large impressive bookshop and inquired on his behalf for the *Sahaj Path*. The pert, officious little salesman pretended that there might be such a text in the back, went off for ten minutes, and then appeared with an armful of alternatives. But no *Natural Learning*. Logan smiled wryly, determined to have that precise book. He bought himself the complete works of Shakespeare instead and offered to buy Gokhale a book if he wanted. Gokhale demurred, politely. They proceeded therefore to another shop and on the way passed a record store. To Logan's amazement the sounds of *Santana,* an American jazz-rock group, were booming forth. Excitedly he pulled Gokhale into the store and together the two of them looked through the hundred or so LPs on display.

'Electric jazz,' whispered Logan, in a sort of trance. 'Look, there's Miles Davis' *Bitches Brew!* In Calcutta... !'

Gokhale who clearly didn't understand this astonishment of Logan's, asked politely about this Mr Miles Davis. He stared in great surprise at the bright and startling psychedelic design on the LP cover.

'You are so *mentally* different,' he concluded very earnestly, 'from us Indians. You Americans and you English.'

Eventually they stepped back into the sunshine. It was a burning sickly heat by early afternoon. Without fair warning

9

Logan then had the fright of his life. For he was met by the apparition of the *hacked torso* of a child. Just a head and a body. No arms. No legs. Rolling... like some self-propelling barrel down the pavement. A child with all his limbs removed. A human barrel. And behold he was singing. He was singing very gaily, like a bird. In a sweet, sharp, childish voice.

'Hare Krishna, Hare Krishna, Hare Rama...'

There arose tender cooes and wondering oohs from the passers-by. Rich Indians stopped for once and tossed paise coins into a nearby cloth. The little ten-year-old torso rolled backwards and forwards, to and from his stationary radial point, his scrappy little collection cloth.

'Christ!' went the blasphemous young Englishman to the Christian's obvious pained endurance. Logan stood frozen with the pained imbecility of all gauche westerners. Yet he hadn't seen quite all. About five yards off, sat an old, old man who also had no legs, yet had kept possession of both his arms. The old man gazed at the barrel-child sulkily. At every paise toss he winced. He was moaning something in just audible Bengali.

'What is he saying?' Logan asked Gokhale. 'What's that old beggar mumbling there, George?'

'That the child is a very great nuisance. For all the adult beggars...'

'Really? Is that all?'

Gokhale bashfully whispered exactly what the legless old man was saying and Logan smiled in a frozen way. He threw two rupees into the cloth of the barrel-child and then walked over to the old man. He put ten rupees into his empty hands. Then there was an indignant cry to his left, for a window-gazing woman had obscured from sight a second old beggar who had relinquished his two arms but kept both his withered legs. Logan walked over and put another ten rupees into his piece of cloth. He received the Hindu benedictions in silence. For some reason he winked as to a grandfather at that second aged beggar.

'I spent thirty-five rupees on Shakespeare,' he explained to tutting Gokhale. 'Where would he have been without *his* arms?'

10

Some joke. In fact he was in a state of shock, combined with a weary fatigue at Gokhale's dreary company. He could not blink out the sight of that rolling torso of a child. Gokhale explained calmly that such beggars had been thus maimed from childhood, by their parents, a delicate decision when the alternative was for the family to starve. Logan looked about him at the faces of the stretching row of beggars, some merely, merely blind, or a trifle, trifle hunchbacked... and on all of them that sad, pained but essentially passive and accepting suffering. He was filled with such hopeless gloom that he felt quite mad and quite light-headed. In fact it was just as he felt ready to sit down on the pavement and start begging himself in some obscure mimetic sympathy, that he caught sight of a luscious, enormous Italian cake shop...

His comforts! In at once he dragged Gokhale who watched politely as Mr Logan bought them both massive Italian cream cakes. The friendly young baker smiled at them in an admiring way and bashfully lamented that his Italian cake shop - he was himself a Bengali - was about to close very soon because of lack of customers. No one knew a good cake from a bad cake these days, he grieved. Logan guzzled down his confection in two seconds flat. Gokhale hesitated, then clumsily spread cream and pastry all over his mouth as he nibbled away at a snail's pace...

They left *Firpo's* and proceeded further in the railway station direction. To their left was a cinema, a large old, imperial-style cinema. Idly Logan stared up at the billboards. Then beheld, to his further stupefaction, the sight of two British household faces, two television stars of weary, childhood, Saturday evening excesses of television gaping.

'Roy Castle,' he mumbled to Gokhale. 'Roy Castle and Alan Freeman. Starring in *Doctor Terror's House Of Horrors...*'

It was beyond Gokhale, the tourist's stiff amazement. Logan explained to him the mad incongruity of coming across an ancient English B-movie, the soundtrack in English and no Bengali subtitles apparently, with film stars of the calibre of these television personalities, these childrens' favourites.

11

Gokhale nodded politely but it was plain he misunderstood his friend's surprise. He imagined that Logan was simply touched to see his own country represented thus in such a distant land. Logan by now felt totally indifferent towards George Gokhale's problems. He reflected drearily that George would be ready to tag along with him for the rest of his stay in Calcutta and not out of any particular leeching nor selfish propensity, but simply because it was a way of passing his hopeless and infinitely foreseeable time. Gokhale had four limbs but no one wanted to employ them full-time to any advantage. Gokhale's heart did not bleed for the limbless beggars. No more than the beggars' hearts bled for the beggars. Logan made out a Naxalite scrawl in English on a distant wall. That was the forbidden word, those terrible revolutionaries, assassins whom the police and government were doing their best to flatten into silence. Logan just didn't know what to think next when faced by all these parallel and never converging hopelessnesses. He didn't know what to think next, never mind what on earth to do next. Should he make yet another search for his *Sahaj Path?*

'Let's go into the cinema,' he suggested blindly, 'to see *Doctor Terror's House Of Horrors!* I want to show you *our* street performers, Mr Gokhale.'

After some hesitation, George assented. They ascended to the balcony of a truly English cinema, replete with pop corn and ice-cream. They sat and stared for ninety minutes at one of the worst films ever made. Alan Freeman was attacked by a strangulating plant. Roy Castle was seized by the Haitian voodoo. The well-heeled though rather small audience all gasped with horror at the appropriate moments. The Indians it seemed to Logan had a different sense of horror, as well as of eye-contact. Gokhale was as frightened as much as anyone. Logan almost fell asleep. Just as he was about to nod off, the little limbless beggar appeared to his inner eyes, this time singing in a cheeky, cockneyed, English television, light-variety manner.

'Roll out the barrel
Roll out the barrel...'

After the film Logan left Gokhale rather sharply, as his company and his evangelical conversation were getting beyond his pitiful patience. He thought Gokhale might have called something after him but he chose to ignore it. He returned to his hotel, a dusty barn of a place on a tenement's third floor, essentially one very large room containing a dozen bunk beds. At its far right end was the bathroom, the lavatory bowl always choked with faeces as the water was always being cut off at this time of the year. Sprawled on the dozen beds were various young travellers of both sexes; a rather strange Australian girl who slithered into her nightdress with arousing twists and turns of her limbs; a dour, obese, humourless German called Ruprecht who had his massive left arm in a sling. Alone the fat youth had been around the empty wilds of Kashmir on horseback. Recently he had been hotly pursued over a high brick wall by the Indian police, and hence his broken left arm. Also, a friendly and cynical Canadian called Bill, who had not washed his long taggy hair for three and a half months. And a sitar-playing, pensive young genius called Ad who hailed from Tilburg, Holland.

And the remarkable hotelier, seated at a desk outside the door to the dormitory. He was Anglo-Indian and was burly, handsome and quite crazy. About fifty-five or so he was a very obvious drunkard and a rabid Hindu nationalist to boot. His voice was regal and superior, his manner rhetorical, bantering and more or less contemptuous. His prices too were exorbitant for the services limply offered.

'My friend,' he coughed sardonically, as Logan made to whip past him. 'You are happily relishing the Calcutta sights? With a clutch of scholarly books I descry? Would you kindly allow me to inspect such treasures?'

Logan halted and warily handed over his Nabokov, Shakespeare, Huxley and Koestler.

'A wise German,' sneered Mr Chatterjee of the last.

'Hungarian,' corrected Logan heartlessly.

'Do you speak it?' bantered Chatterjee with narrowed eyes.

'Hungarian? No, but I speak a little German.'

'German I mean of course!' said the manager with a hiccup.

13

'I speak French, German, Italian and... Swedish.'

Logan pursed his lips, hoping false impressment would hasten his departure from the desk here.

'Listen,' said Chatterjee, standing up and flicking his head histrionically, 'I shall speak some German for you. "Ish vull gippish bander nikk farden..."' ... and a great deal more of the same gibberish followed.

Then. 'You translate!' barked Chatterjee like Logan's old headmaster.

'I'm afraid I didn't understand a word,' admitted Logan expressionlessly.

'Hah!' sneered handsome Chatterjee. 'Clearly you are no great linguist, Herr Logan!'

Not content with proving Logan's linguistic ignorance he pulled him over to a painting which hung behind his desk, a framed devotional picture of some Vaishnava saint, who smiled at them both with a smoky-eyed benignity.

'Chaitanya,' said wild Chatterjee with tears in the eyes of his very European face. 'Lord Chaitanya who was the saint of all saints! Do you know that when I stare into the eyes of this picture here, Mr Logan, my eyes start to fill up with compassion, which is to say God in his kindest, most human form. And those tears which wash my soul and purify me thereby cause me to be made like to God' - here he had to stop himself tottering he was so drunk - 'And when my soul is thus cleansed I am as pure as Lord Bishnoo's greatest devotee, Lord Chaitanya...'

'So why do you drink so much?' asked Logan, after a pause.

'What!' gasped Chatterjee, staggering. 'I do not drink! Or... oh well, yes, to be sure, to your eyes, your *naive* western mind it must appear so! But it is not I that do the drinking. It is my *body* that does the drinking! My body drinks and maybe sometimes it even gets drunk. But I, my soul, the Lord Chaitanya devotee, I am a *jeevan-mukta,* a released-in-life, the body does not shackle me for I have restrained my senses like a charioteer his horses as is described in the beautiful *Gita.* And remember, Mr Logan, it is *karuna,* compassion, which is the

14

essence of my eternal soul.'

So concluding, he sank back, wheezing, into his chair. Logan made to depart. Just as he did, the tea-boy came and asked Mr Chatterjee for some order, and the manager angrily roared and bellowed at him in the unmistakable innocence of his time-bound, drunken, though merely bodily self.

Days went by. The tense and also bored-looking Australian girl borrowed one of Logan's novels. They became friendly companions of a sort. One evening the two of them smoked some hashish and listened to the Dutchman tell them all he knew about *Madhyamika* Buddhism. The cynical Canadian, strangely attentive when it came to Indian thought, also joined the circle. Outside their dormitory the landlord was singing a fierce devotional hymn to Bishnoo. Outside their window it was noisy, riotous festival time. The Dutchman talked non-stop for about three hours and whether it was the effect of the *ganja* or not, it seemed to Logan that the man from Tilburg was far from being a dilettante. Apart from the sitar he had taught himself Sanskrit, Tibetan and *Old* Bengali. His erudition seemed quite phenomenal. He spoke in an English so very articulate it made Ruprecht the one-armed equestrian very obviously jealous.

Just as Logan was about to doze off on his bed, the tea-boy entered and indicated to the Englishman he had a message for him. The servant was bashful, timid of walking into the European circle. Logan staggered his way over and clapped him on the shoulder in a brotherly way.

'What is it?'

'A man, sahib. From the streets. He wishes to see you.'

'Who on earth can that be?'

The boy pointed to the half open door and there on the stairs sat a nervous-looking Gokhale. Logan flinched with disappointment. Gokhale saw Logan's disappointment. Logan saw Gokhale watching the foreigner's antipathy and an infinitely serial shame rebounded between and independent of the two. It was the pitiless deity of embarrassment.

'Oh... hallo,' murmured Logan limply, as he walked out onto

the staircase. Mr Chatterjee had finally fallen asleep, handsomer than ever, after his vocal devotions.

'Hallo, Mr Logan. I came to see you.'

'Oh...' mumbled the Englishman.

Logan was stupefied, the hashish had left him fuddled and brainless, incapable of sober civilities. Gokhale looked frightened and embarrassed. He coughed and this time it was a regal, a full-throated cough.

'Christ, that sounds bad,' muttered Logan dopily.

'It is,' admitted Gokhale, having winced at Logan's blasphemy, that name so easily taken in vain. 'I borrowed a little money to see a doctor. It is tuberculosis, Mr Logan.'

'Christ,' said Logan.

'Hark,' coughed Gokhale, wincing again at the name so lightly bandied.

'What... what will you do?' Logan stammered. 'Will you get some treatment?'

Gokhale smiled wryly but unaccusingly. Logan sobered just a little. The salient point was of course cash, the fictive paper that came so easily to Europeans and that so brilliantly eluded the hands of nine tenths of Orientals. Through his haze young Logan tried to work out whether it was a financial touch or not. Or what the devil was it? What was it? Horrifyingly, even through his dope, even on this slipway to Gokhale's survival or expiry, Logan found George Gokhale totally *boring...*

He pondered incoherently. Even if it was a touch, it was only right, it was only just. If for example Logan had had TB and no money to see a doctor, then by God he ought to have gone and demanded it off anyone who had money galore, who had rupees and paise by the thousand...

However... however... he reflected, only this afternoon he had calculated he had just enough money - sixteen hundred rupees - to get himself back to England if he was to travel by train and coach overland. He had exactly ninety pounds in rupees while the cheapest air ticket cost one hundred pounds. The weary overland haul he viewed with little relish, yet even that he could just afford. If he now gave Gokhale some of his meagre cash he was simply stuck fast here in Calcutta, as penniless as those pathetic French morphine addicts who begged on the streets alongside the native beggars. Unless, fuzzily he thought, he were to have a quick whip-round in the 'hotel' here. He turned. He stared at the stoned, tranquil faces all clustered round the Dutchman explaining the *shunya* void in all its inexplicability. Somehow... he somehow thought not.

He changed the subject. He hated George Gokhale and wished he were back in England away from all this bloody *death*. He talked of the Civic Museum. George did not seem all that surprised, neither by Logan's druggedness nor his keeping him here at the staircase top. More than anything he looked concerned for Logan, as if fearful at his entanglement with the people there inside the dormitory.

As their conversation trickled out, Logan eventually made some excuses, his fatigue, a hard day of traipsing around the enormous Civic Museum. Mr Gokhale coughed, coughed his death hack, as Mr Logan explained to him his traveller's fatigue. Gokhale hid his cough as best he might, his skinny face contorted into something as repulsive in its dog-hanging way as it was piteous. The little Christian turned and trudged his way downstairs, forgiving the European all the way down. The European quickly invented excuses, as he followed on, tacitly forgave Gokhale his embarrassment, as he tried to talk both of them out of their grave shames and unspeakable difficulties.

Back in the dormitory, he buried. himself in Koestler, the tale about the man who had psychologically lost the use of his legs. He wondered dazedly if Koestler had ever thought of making it the... He, Logan, needed to go home. He, Gokhale, needed to live. He, Logan, had no rich parents, no rich friends to bail him out of penury. He, Gokhale, would view Logan's poor parents, poor friends, as millionaires if he were to hear of their circumstances. The banality of it, the mad questions. How could he help every dying Indian when they hacked off their legs and hacked up their babies for... when the buggers didn't even bloody *mind* that they were all starving and dying and all to no purpose?

Logan took pains to avoid George Gokhale for the rest of his time in Calcutta. He paid the tea-boy a few rupees to say to the Christian that he was always out. He and the Australian woman spent a fair amount of time in excellent Chinese restaurants. He checked with the boy, after a week, and discovered that the thin little man, the one who coughed, had been back four or five times, the last time mentioning something about a favour - what was not clear - about something that he needed. Logan flushed and loudly groaned. The tea-boy stared at him. He personally abominated the little rat-faced Indian Christian and would have gladly kicked him down the stairs. Logan explained to the tea-boy that the man was in need of a doctor and had no money and the favour he asked must have been for some money to go and prevent his own death. He was only about thirty-five. Jesus Christ, he exclaimed, aloud to the tea-boy. Thirty-five! The tea-boy's English was not very good but he smiled politely at the boring explanation. Logan now often took a rear exit from the hotel to avoid the possible approach of George Gokhale. He would have hidden in a dustbin had it been necessary.

He left for Delhi, and further west, on the following Wednesday. Happy to be departing, he took the Canadian and the Australian girl out for a meal on that last Tuesday evening. In the restaurant the three of them discussed at length the *Madhyamika* Buddhism as propounded by Ad the Dutchman. They also talked about Indian cities and the phenomenon of hustling, the eternal bothering for money or for time or for something. The Canadian spoke with approval of the kingdom of Nepal where they were even poorer (the average wage in 1973 was sixty pence a week) but where for some reason beggary was almost nil. The Australian girl remarked that she was flying to Thailand in a week's time. She had a traveller's sparkle in her lovely eyes. Both Logan and the Canadian wanted very much to sleep with her but there was no way of doing so in their communal boudoir. Unless it was effected in the bathroom, next to the choked, insanitary lavatory. She had such glorious breasts, thought hungry Logan, she had such trembling brilliant curves.

18

'It must simply be the physical space,' he murmured at last. 'All that free space in Nepal. They aren't as frantic, even if they're poorer. And of course there aren't so many of them. Here there are millions, millions, millions...'

The Canadian was still puzzling out *Madhyamika* Buddhism, the notion of no-thingness.

'If neither the mind is real, nor what the mind perceives is real. If everything is ideal and only the Void, No-thingness, has any... reality...'

'Then give me these *ideal* lamb cutlets,' exclaimed the Australian girl, dabbing at the succulent juices on her plate, her nose twinkling anarchically. 'And bugger the Void. I don't mind if they aren't real. I don't mind. I don't give a damn, I don't really.'

With bloated stomachs they staggered back to the hotel. The tea-boy was there making the sleeping genius Mr Chatterjee a refreshing beverage. Logan smiled at the servant and headed for the dormitory.

But the tea-boy hastily pursued him, murmuring gently and holding in his hand a paper bag that was wrapped with some raggy-looking string.

'The favour, sahib,' he whispered, trying not to awaken Chatterjee from his Vaishnavite dreams.

'Whose?' asked Logan, a little drunk himself for once.

'Krishtian. Krishtian favour.'

Logan all but reeled.

'Christ!' - he heard in his head George Gokhale dismally wincing - 'What the hell is this?'

As if he didn't know. The tea-boy smiled patiently and went back to his sleeping master. The Australian and the Canadian stared amused at the pathetic-looking package.

'What is *that?*' asked the plump girl in a lively way. 'Is it some jewels you've had cut price from the King of Sikkim?'

'No,' muttered Logan, as he fingered the bindings and the leaves inside the grey little parcel. 'It's *Natural Learning* is what it is. George Gokhale must have found some copies. It's from George Gokhale and I don't expect I'll see him to say goodbye tomorrow morning.'

Those Who Scorn Sir Walter Scott

Former farmhand Frankie Chives, eighty-one next birthday, was
brought back by a Panda car after a seasonable hitch-hike all the
way to Birmingham. Whereupon Mr Gowls instructed Mercy to
wrest him from his wooden leg and secure him in the safety of a
wheelchair. Which Mercy accomplished with her usual friendly
chaffing. People who work in Old Folks' Homes usually banter
and maintain themselves this way. Head of Home Gowls was a
bluffer category: soldierish exterior, dark moustache, dry and
sarcastic, yet kind and conscientious underneath. Frankie
suspected that he entertained impassioned desires for Mercy,
although he was sixty-one and married and she was thirty-two
and single. Gowls looked like a walrus, Mercy like a slow,
wide-eyed seal. Frankie did not see himself in an animal light,
unless it was in terms of character as a fox, wolf, sly dog, what
have you...

In fact he looked like a shrivelled old goat. His face was
white and blotched with pale freckles. He was wrinkled and old.
He was as old as old can be. He had only one leg and was now
thrown perforce into the prison of a wheelchair, enduring the
idiot banter of parrot-voiced Mercy and her mumbling about
how they'd all missed him, especially old Dossie who had a
crush on Frankie, and whom Frankie treated with a violent
disdain.

'How on earth did you ever get a lift?' she asked him
humorously as she took away his leg.

'Brains,' spat Frankie. 'What you lack, *Mer-ci-a?*

Mercy chuckled. Compared with the abuse she got from
some of her charges, such candour was mild. Mercy was
mousy-haired, slow-moving, always slightly startled, slightly
hypnotised, slightly strange. For she had had jagged misfortunes
in the past and these always leave their mark.

She put him in the wheelchair, took him round to the back
door of the Home, the double-doored glass portals, as he

requested. She asked him gently if there was anything more she could do for him. Frankie commanded her to fetch him his book from his bedroom upstairs, *Quentin Durward* by Sir Walter Scott. Mercy did his bidding and then repeated her offer. Frankie gave an obscene, unkind retort. The Deputy smiled sweetly, called him a nasty old bugger, and went off to plan rotas with Mr Gowls.

Frankie became filled with melancholy. Then he fell asleep. Then he woke up and screwed his face into recognition of where, when, who etc. He saw outside, not too clearly, the rear of the Old Folks' Home. There was a well-tended lawn, some beds of roses, a slope leading up to flats for the police. For this was a new town, a *new* town in the Midlands. If he had turned round in his chair he would have seen the front of this cubicular building, the same glass doors looking out once more onto lawn, shrubs, saplings tied by leather belts to fence posts to help them grow. Ha, thought Frankie often, to help the young things grow and live.

To his left was Gowls' office. Adjacent to that, next to the recreation room, was the office of the Deputy, Mercy. Behind him and to the left was the dining room. On the other side of the glass front door was a main artery for Midlands traffic, choked with cars and lorries and bleep-bleep zebra crossings. It was quite impossible to cross the road without the use of a zebra crossing, even on a Sunday. Frankie had been a farmhand and remembered trees. This town, the nearest to his village, was nothing but concrete, glass, hypermarkets, Do It Yourself and depots. Birmingham this morning had been worse, completely mad, but beyond there he had expected to find countryside of some description. The Black Country he believed had some countryside to it. The copper had found him wandering round in circles, looking for a way out of The Bullring. Already it was known who he was, the town police had got onto the Brum lads, flashed Mr Chives' description (a bit like a wrinkled old goat with a limp, as Gowls had supplied it), had him taped and knackered before he'd even opened his mouth...

When you are eighty and institutionalised, it is permissible to

21

tell a policeman to go and fuck a donkey. Frankie had this morning several times and half-relished the deed. The young policeman who drove him home had been all sympathy but Frankie had been unimpressed. He told him that his uniform meant nothing to him, it was just a shield and so on. The young man had thought the old man was cracked. The old man had told the young man he too would be dead one day. Finally the young man had returned to his own town, job, his own family, his Edgbaston garden, his own patch you might say. While Frankie was homeless, legless and glued to the glass here like a mongrel that waits for its master to return to give it a five minute walk.

Mollie who was called by Mercy a syko-jerry, staggered to the payphone two yards behind the ex-farmhand's head and without putting in a five pence or a ten pence, for to be sure her mind had stopped making accurate registration of the without as long ago as 1966, began a conversation with her husband Jack, deceased fourteen years ago. She told him his tea was ready and she had made him a flan for pudding. Mollie said it was very hot today, a real sweat heat. Then she gravely added she had worries about all sorts, worries hard to put a finger on. Then she upbraided Jack for being so late these days, always a good hour late for his tea. Then she started to sob and accuse and that really riled old Frankie. He turned round and told her smartly to bugger off, to go and pester somebody else.

'Can't you see I'm trying to read?' he muttered nastily. 'A great book by a great writer. Go and watch kiddies' television, *Mo-lee!*'

Mollie wandered off to the other payphone next to the dining room. Frankie rubbed his eyes, took a sip from the glass of lemonade put there thoughtfully by Mercy for when the old man awoke. The liquid loosened his mouth, swirled around his gums and jaws. It freshened him up. And why not? Didn't remedies always repeat themselves? He opened his novel at a random page and began to read. For his reading technique these days had reached the accomplished master stage of his beginning at completely random points. Frankie loved books so much he did not give a damn for their plots. He loved Sir Walter's prose so much it was irrelevant to him where he started or finished, whether he read the same bit thrice or thirty times. Ten years ago he had usually read his books backwards, reading the chapters in reverse order that is. Now he just dipped, read, savoured, closed, opened, dipped, savoured and so forth. It was as if he were a wine taster. Also he read aloud, with dramatic, contemptuous declamation. He knew for a fact Gowls and Mercy never read a book. They hadn't the wits. Yet so as not to share, nor pollute nor weaken his private talisman, old Frankie read his book just loud enough for anyone almost to get the drift, but not enough for them to actually do so.

Thus, just as Mercy passed by on her way to the Ladies, Frankie muttered aggressively, half-audibly:

'It is all the better,' said Quentin to himself, his spirit rising with the apprehended difficulties of his situation; 'that lovely young lady shall owe all to me - What one hand- ay, and one head can do, - methinks I can boldly count upon...'

He broke off wilfully as he felt Mercy pause to take in his delivery. 'And boldly count upon fried onions and fast young doctors ,' he improvised much more loudly. 'And nosey Noras poking their snouts up till the moon and back, methinks!'

The Deputy flushed and dived into the lavatory. Not simply on account of Frankie. For just at that moment the back doors opened and the doctor to the Old Folks' Home made entrance. He was a tall, rather hasty-gestured man in his early forties. His name was Meadows and he was enjoying a crudely disguised affair with Mercy. For he was married with three children and spent approximately five times more hours than he should have spent at this institution. Meadows didn't even notice Frankie reading aloud, nor that he was now in a wheelchair where once he had hobbled about on an artificial leg. He looked up the stairs to Mercy's flat - the Deputy lived on the premises, while the Head lived twenty miles away in Towcester - and made straight for the empty love nest. For some reason he was quite fearless about his philandering. People surmised that his wife rarely left their large white house which lay on the other side of town. He walked into Mercy's bed with the same professional curtness and briskness as he did into dying old peoples' chambers.

Another door opened. The Head of Home chose just then to leave his room. He paused, nodded to the doctor expressionlessly, and continued sharply en route to the dining room. Even Frankie saw that Gowls was jealous of the doctor. The Head of Home disguised it as disapproval at the fate of the doctor's poor wife and of the professional man's exploitation of gullible, trusting Mercy. As far as Gowls was concerned, he wasn't a particularly *kindly* philanderer, wasn't that superior, chisel-faced medical man...

From the Ladies Mercy returned with haste to the main area of reception. She halted, coughed, pretended to be suddenly struck by something, and then dashed up the stairs as if to fetch it, whatever it was.

'Shame! shame! Arnot!' said Lord Crawford, 'a soldier on duty should say nought of what he sees...' continued the old man louder than ever as he sensed the Deputy's guilty retreat.

Overnight one-legged Frankie planned his next stratagem. He sat up in bed smoking away at his Woodbines Tipped, the white-tipped ones that have so much flavour they seem to rend holes in your cheeks. Smoking was forbidden in the bedrooms for obvious reasons: age, sleep, sedatives and so on. Frankie sat up, propped on his pillows, and read away at *Quentin Durward* and in between orations he paused and contemplated the best means of escape. The criminals had his wooden leg and refused to return it to him. He wondered if Wilf the handyman could make him a substitute out of a clothes pole or similar. Cut to size, tied at the stump with a bit of cord. Or maybe he could make it himself if he wheeled out one day in his chair with the pretence of enjoying this fine July weather.

The next day brought entertainments and with them an even greater urge in Frankie Chives to tear himself from the joys of being among his own age group. Yesterday's young lorry driver had been more to Frankie's taste. He had had a filthy tongue and a feast of tantalising stories about his female hitch-hikers. They were mostly invented of course, but then so was *Quentin Durward.* Today they had plonked him, against his will, in the front row of the recreation room, for from 11.00 to 12.30, two folk singers from the local Baptist Youth Club had promised to entertain the old people. The man was about twenty-five, tall, scrawny and full of patter, the way folk singers usually resolve. Today he was among the aged so his patter was correspondingly more lengthy and intimate and unambiguous. His wife was likely a couple of years younger and she was vast in the breast and full of smile and broad of humour. About six out of the twenty-five present seemed to derive any pleasure from the performance. Mercy who was supervising was naturally doing the rounds and urging them all to clap, join the refrains and show a bit of gratitude to this generous, unpaid young couple.

'*Kumbayawa kumbaya,*' sang the selfless couple, too loud for Frankie's taste.

'*Kumbayawa kumbaya,*' echoed kind Mercy, with all her zest and optimism.

'Come on, Frankie Chives,' she added, shouting to his back from the back. 'Give us a refrain, old man...'

Dossie turned down her hearing aid and sank into a kind of coma. Her friend Madge said at the top of her voice (for she was also a little deaf): '*This is of no interest to us...*'

There had been a pause for the refrain just then and Madge's candour filled it in very neatly and crisply. The young singers felt their mouths go loose and waxy. Mercy sang the louder to drown it all. Frankie snorted and cleared his throat, hawked loud enough to make the wood in the girl's Spanish guitar vibrate.

Frankie was ready for his lunch when all was said and done. Which at the Home began at twelve thirty-five but the old folk liked to go to the lavatory, wash their hands for instance, for the twenty minutes before. Thus at twelve-ten, twenty minutes before the end of the show, Frankie turned and pushed for the door and went right across the path of the singers bashing out *Michael Rows The Boat Ashore.* Mercy fumed and with gestures of embarrassment admonished him from the back. Frankie muttered whore - there was no mistaking it - and then giggled, continuing his stony path towards the dining room. Dossie rose, adjusted her hearing aid, and followed her hero in the wheelchair. Madge followed immediately behind furiously reiterating that that had been of *no* interest to them. Two dozen old folk were renouncing art in favour of fodder and Mercy was disgusted. Soon all but she and three of the most helpless had left the folk singers hallooing to themselves and their Lord.

Two hours later we find Gowls in a quandary, or fairer to say in one of more than half a dozen, as he broods inside his cubicle-office. Gowls is the worrying type, his accomplishments are a function of the vigorous whittling away of his numerous anxieties. He has the soldierly stance with good reason as he has been - in his twenties - an officer in the Coldstream Guards. He was not a toff officer, is his frequent boast, but the son of a Brackley fruiterer made it from the ranks. He has a brisk, dry manner, a markedly provincial accent, that endears him to all but nincompoops and the most bonelessly posh. Anxiety number one pertains to his age and his sex and the lack of it in relishable measure at this stage. Number two that he might one day make a fool of himself by grabbing at Mercy and getting slapped for his pains. Number three that Frankie's rise-and-fall mumbling from Sir Walter Scott three yards away from his door, direly exacerbates all his other concerns. Number four that in seven days time he has been commanded by the County Office to perform the utterly impossible...

The memorandum from the Health and Safety Officer (the Horseshit and Sheepshit Offerer was his soubriquet according to Gowls) was demanding that the Old People's Home should perform a fire drill, a *full* fire drill next Thursday, the 17th of July. After which - there had to be a report submitted by Gowls as to its efficacy, efficiency, efficacity, all those sort of words. Notwithstanding, as far as the ex-officer was concerned, such a snap demand was cruel and absurd. By a full fire drill was meant, on paper, the deafening ringing of the electric bell, the brisk alerting of the thirty-odd geriatric residents, the interesting pause while time passed and they were hungrily awaited out on the lawn at the back by the half dozen staff here. The H.S.O. was apparently envisaging such a painless practice once every six months - for starters.

Gowls grimaced at the amateur impracticality of the vision of the County Hall bureaucrat. These residents were not schoolchildren with alert wits, restless feet and fidgety eagerness to please the handsome young teacher. No, they were eighty-year-old Madge, eighty-eight-year-old Dossie, eighty-seven-year-old Mollie, eighty-year-old Frankie and twenty-five similar or twice as bad. To expect them to jump to a dire imperative was to expect them to comprehend Boolean algebra. The real job at hand, in the event of an actual fire, would be to drag them protesting and kicking to the back door and then to shove them out with maximum force. Hitherto Gowls' fire drill had been a practicable, accomplishable affair. It had meant for Gowls and Mercy simply training the staff to *simulate* the drill, late at night, when all the residents were asleep. For Mercy to *pretend* to clear residents out of B Block Upper, Gowls likewise B Block Lower, the rest of the place by the other four Care Assistants, Gowls and Mercy then leading the way around any possible crannies where one or two somnambulists and psychogeriatrics had hypothetically secreted themselves.

'It was troublesome at first,' said Durward, *'but became more easy by use, and I was weak with my wounds and loss of blood, and desirous to gratify my preserver...'* came from outside his half-open door.

'Christ,' snorted Gowls from his office, with fetid irritation. 'And what happens in winter, in February full fire drill? When they're stood outside on that lawn there, blue with cold?'

'Bring him forward,' said the king, *'place the man before my face who dares maintain these palpable falsehoods.'*

The doors swung open and tall insatiable Doctor Meadows entered, his face alert and hungry with the intimations of this afternoon's clandestine wickedness.

'Christ!' was audible once more from Gowls' half-open door.

Meadows raised his eyebrows and his comic expression happened to settle on Frankie. Frankie stared at Doctor Meadows, then through him with transfixing disdain.

'Pimp,' he croaked at the leech.

'What!'

Frankie turned to Scott and read with unusual audibility, '*I regard not your foul suspicions,' replied Quentin, 'my duty is plain and peremptory - to convey these ladies in safety to Liège...*'

Meadows shrugged and passed on up the stairs to Mercy's flat. Not without noting that Gowls had appeared at the door just in time to hear that bizarre accusation from that ugly little man in the wheelchair. Fortunately he was not to observe Gowls winking conspiratorially at Frankie nor unfortunately allow himself what would have been the pleasure at Frankie's response to the overture from Gowls.

'You're another...' grumbled the ex-farmhand, avoider of both World Wars.

'What?' inquired soldier Gowls, losing his smile most swiftly.

'A pimp. A pimp, a varlet and a knave to beat all knavery, methinks.'

When Thursday morning came it was even worse than Gowls had expected. At ten-twenty-five the cherry-faced Deputy went roaring into the Recreation Room simultaneous with the horrendous ringing of the fire bell. For full authenticity the Head of Home had made it so that the residents had to believe there actually was a fire just then.

'Fire, fire! We're on fire, old people!' she cried with the gusto of a volcano itself.

A good two-thirds of the residents were sitting there in that one room, convenience itself had a fire been genuine. They all stared at Mercy as if she were crazy. Dossie turned down her hearing aid and resumed her gentle dozing. Madge told the

Deputy to shut her mouth, as she couldn't hear herself think just then.

'But there's a fire!' implored Mercy indignantly. 'This Home is on fire and you're all going to go up in smoke! Come on! Get out onto the lawn at the back there!'

They stared at her unmoved. Most of them shook their heads in blatant disbelief. Mercy mortified, while Gowls watched it all from the door with satisfaction. Then, as rehearsed, two of the Care Assistants came bursting in and roared and bawled like Mercy did, testifying in tongues to the existence and the power of the encroaching conflagration.

Seal-eyed Mercy breathed easier as she saw one or two of them make a move. Then, horrified, she observed Dossie moving in the direction of what should have been the flaming stairs.

'Where are *you* sneaking off, Dossie?' she shrieked. 'That's where the bloody fire is - upstairs!'

Dossie paid no heed. She muttered that she had her *things* upstairs and she wanted them *things,* fire or no fire. She had her pools coupons and her sweets up there in her bedroom...

'And where the hell are *you* off, Cynthia Sellars?'

Cynthia Sellars was hobbling upstairs for her cardigan. Even though it was July and roasting she refused to step outside without her knitted cardigan.

'But you'll be burnt alive!' cautioned one of the Assistants.

'Good,' grunted Cynthia, stonily.

As Gowls had foreseen it was a question of dragging, shoving and bullying them to save their miserable old lives. He himself had to put several old ladies across his back and bear them out with authentic firemen's lifts. One of them struck his ear with her upraised crutch. Another sank her withered old teeth into his shoulder. Mercy had to put old Jim's arms behind his back and threaten to twist them if he wouldn't go and save his bloody old life. Some had to be woken and dragged down the stairs in their nighties and pyjamas. Some became incontinent all over Gowls' shoulders. Some who were successfully put outside on the lawn started to feel cold - even in this ridiculous July heat - and walked back into the Home again. They walked back into the flames, like *suttees*. They had to be rescued twice!

When Frankie saw what was going on he sniffed victoriously and wheeled himself into the alcove next to the payphone. He hoped in this way to remain unobserved and aloof from this fool charade. For he had heard Gowls' verbal protest the same day he'd received that irritating memo from the H.S.O. Frankie knew this was all fake and was damned if he was going to renounce his favourite place just to go and sit surrounded out there on the lawn by weeping Mollie, wandering Dossie, crazy Madge and swearing Arthur...

Finally his absence out there on the back lawn became apparent to Mercy, she who was the hub and the nerve centre of the Old Folks' Home. Despite unhinging adultery and over-indulgence in strong white wine, Mercy did her job, such as it was, to perfection.

'Where's Frankie?' she shouted at the thirty sweating, shivering, squinting, dribbling, silent, raving, alert, wooden, impressive, ludicrous old people.

'Where's Jack?' beseeched Mollie the syko-jerry. 'Where's my husband, Jackie?'

'Where's Frankie?' echoed Dossie, who had just turned up her hearing aid. 'I love him, I *love* Frankie Chives.'

Gowls put his hand out and stopped impassioned old Dossie from flinging herself into the putative inferno. Just then one of the Care Assistants spotted him skulking in the alcove and pointed him out to the colourful assembly.

'You!' went Mercy as she strode through the doors and made for the alcove. 'Come on!' she commanded sternly to the old man who was already bent deeply into his novel.

'*Blessed Mother of Mercy! thou who art omnipotent with Omnipotence, have compassion with me as a sinner!*' Frankie sneered.

'Pronto,' urged Mercy amiably. 'Or do you want to go up in smoke like a real sinner?'

'Bollicks!' snapped Frankie ruthlessly, putting aside his

ancient volume. 'Tell the truth for once. All of youse! There ain't no bloody fire. There ain't one, I know for a wondrous dowry.'

'There is!' insisted the Deputy. 'What do you think all of us except you is doing stood out on the back lawn, Frankie Chives?'

'Foolishness! Folly! I heard him, *Gow-ells,* rigging the whole thing with County. It's a rig, a practice, and *Gow-ells* thinks it's all horseshit too. I know that for pursuivant verity! Go to! For shame! Nay! *Pasques-dieu!* Stop lying all you lot! Doctors poking more than appendixes, thou jade! Old Gowls wanting his twopenny worth or I'm a brigand. What goes on up them stairs is a pretty conceit I trow, *Mer-ci-a!'*

Mercy, who had sinned so much in the past and disbelieved her own deeds so utterly, who refused to admit that the honest, straightforward person she was could have married, gone wild, separated and left her one little girl with another woman, and now be embarrassing the doctor's wife and children... all of that and all from kind, simple, faithful Mercy whose eyes stared panickingly froglike with disbelief at her own deeds... Mercy now cursed at the vicious old man and dragged him out roughly in his wheelchair, out there into the sunshine with the rest of them.

Just then Doctor Meadows came jaunting down the incline on his bicycle, one of those low-slung Moped affairs that look so peculiar under adults. Frankie burst into mocking, noisy laughter while Gowls suppressed a grin or two. Mercy didn't know where to put her face and she dashed off into the almost incinerated wreckage with the excuse of going to the lavatory.

Frankie's intemperate accusations were Mercy's conscience put through loudspeakers. Contrition tends to come when one's sex is spent and that afternoon, after a particularly fierce and loveless coition, Mercy found herself disclosing to Doctor Meadows her doubts and remorse when it came to committing adultery. This ruffled the naked, blood-coloured medical man more than he cared to be. Who enjoys an affair with someone

31

who takes to prating about the sufferings of one's faceless wife and children? It was bad practice and Meadows was depressed. He took the bold step of leaving Mercy's flat two hours earlier than usual and saying coldly that she would have to ring him up if ever she wanted to try her conscience any more. He was damned if he was going to trot up these stairs for *this* three times a week. Which left vulnerable Mercy in a sorry mess, a tearful state. She almost wanted to die, to disappear, to leave the face of the earth. And yet her job had to go on, work and old people still croaked on, still lived and wanted and made their constant, peremptory demands. The past swam up as she wiped her face of tears, her open, glazed, wide and fear-struck mien. For she was thirty-two, twice the philanderess, once with child, twice renounced her child...

She took the evening off, survived the afternoon in the dining room as best as she could, and spent the evening moping in her flat. In her sitting room she kept a tank full of guppies, glaucous-eyed and blameless in their gawkiness. She felt as if about to succumb to a charitable illness, a touch of influenza which would blank her out for a week or so. Mr Gowls, one of the other members of staff on duty tonight, had been most paternal and tender when she'd excused herself from work this evening - unless of course emergencies arose. There was Deirdre the new West Indian Care Assistant patrolling the bedrooms and corridors. Gowls was presently down in his office, unknown to Mercy dreaming up spurious reasons for coming up to her flat. A thermometer, an orange, a lemon perhaps? He was rehearsing his panegyric of her virtues (indispensable right-hand Deputy, her energy, her zest, her cheerfulness, that indefinable special quality that was worth three times the salary she was paid...) full of rehearsed repartee about the stupidity of the H.S.O. and how he'd rubbed the man's nose in it with a four-page report on the success - hah! - of this morning's full fire drill... !

Around nine o'clock Mercy was at her lowest point of self-esteem, toying with the original idea of phoning up Mrs Meadows to say how genuinely sorry she was, really pained, more pained than pleasured, but did she mind if Mercy kept on being visited by her husband because it was such a strong and sincere attachment there was no honourable way out except to get the damaged party's permission, so to speak? Then - there was a knock, and something of a clamour at the door to Mercy's flat...

She opened it anxiously to Deirdre the West Indian girl who stood there quivering with tears and a look of furious anger. She blurted out to the Deputy that that horrible old Frankie Chives was sat up in bed cheekily smoking a smelly old cigarette, reading aloud like a maniac *this book,* resisting all attempts Deirdre made to remove the obvious fire hazard. When Deirdre had scolded him that Gowls' full fire drill might have to be put into practice that very night, and all because of him, Frankie had started to bellow obscenely and called outraged Deirdre a stupid darkie, subsequently a nosey nigger, finally a bitch of a bleeding blackie.

That did it. Mercy rose from the grave and pounded the quarter of a mile to the far end of B Block where resided Mr Chives and his complete collection of the works of Sir Walter and the remains of fifty packs of Woodbine Tipped all shredded and poked into a hideous yet hollow pot ornament. She flung open the door and strode without fear to the grinning old man, he who was flourishing with affectation a second Woodbines Tipped, that geriatric who legless as he was could still have others running fit to burst their lungs.

'Frankie!' cried the panting Deputy. 'Give me that fag, you stupid boy! You *stupid boy* abusing the staff here with your cruel old mouth! Me as well this lunchtime! Us who looks after you and gives in to all your stupid, daft whims. You'll set the Home on fire and burn everyone to ashes! Is that really what you want, you old beggar? Me, poor old Mr Gowls, Dossie, Madge... the cats... the guppies... *everything* inside these four walls here?'

'It would be a positive cheating of Sandie, who is as honest a man who ever tied noose upon hemp... Were I to be hanged myself no other should tie tippet about my craig,' gabbled old

33

Frankie, ostentatiously flicking his ash upon the neat blue counterpane.

'Gimme that cigarette!' bawled Mercy, boldly holding out her palm and tossing her mane like a stallion.

Frankie pulled away his hand and then stabbed it right into the middle of the Deputy's palm. Mercy was to draw away from maiming by as much as an eighth of a second. It took all her resolve not to fetch that hand back across the octogenarian's temples.

Instead she snorted and paced around his bed and muttered: 'Right! Right!'

'On her!' replied Crawford; 'nay if there be a woman in the secret, the Lord ha' mercy, for we are all on the rocks again!'

But the misogynist was to come to a maritime grief, washed up on the moist shores of a lone isle of his damp bed. For wily old Mercy strode calmly over to Frankie's washstand, filled up a beaker with icy water from the tap, turned, stomped back over to Frankie, and flung it all in the direction of the blazing Woodbine.

There was a lengthy phut! Frankie was doused. Deirdre started to laugh and was terrified she'd piss herself. Mercy went into similar convulsions. Frankie gazed down stunned at his novel, the ancient pages already glued fast together...

'You've wet Sir Walter!' he gasped. 'Chrissalmighty... you fish-eyed twat! You ugly frog-faced...'

Frankie was apoplectic. The two women helplessly roared and roared, hysterically, at the thin, wet old man in his wet old fury.

'It took him interteens of years,' protested Frankie with a sincere beseechment in the name of truth. 'It took him years to write *Quentin Durward*. Line after careful line. Page after careful page. All you do is wash old folks' arses and play tussy-tuss with the medicals. You should be ashamed! *Avaunt ye... by my hilts, I am glad of it*. Go away and fu...'

The Care Assistant helpfully deafened herself and went over to change and remake Frankie's bed. Mercy trembled greatly, as earlier today, but covered her blushes by sorting him some new pyjamas. She also took away the dripping novel and promised hoarsely to buy him a new one, a brand new one tomorrow. Frankie had subsided into silence, sulks, deafness, removal from the things of the world. Let's say he was a caliph in a kilt in 1720. He was dead to this present world, this rubbish of plate glass and breeze block and bleep-bleep zebra crossings. He had no money for a farm so he had to farm his imagination. Enough said. He refused to open his mouth. He ignored their apologies, didn't say Good Night, didn't know what it meant and didn't damn well bloody care.

Two hours later Deirdre, a daytime part-timer, has gone home to her husband and family. Mercy who had proceeded straight to Gowls' office to report the incident with Frankie, was still sitting in fertile colloquy with the sympathetic Head of Home. It was late at night, there were just the two of them among an ocean of the sleeping aged. Mercy's heart was sad and her nerves were lonely, and Gowls was a kindly whiskery Daddy, a soldier boy retired, a man of parts. Their voices carried their ponderous solemnities through the queer silence of the deserted corridors outside. All the old ones were fast asleep and it was a fit time for Mercy to unbutton her cares, her curious past, her trials with her marriage, her trials starting today with Doctor Meadows. Gowls' bulbous ears were perfect receptacles. He was aching to encircle young Mercy's shoulders. Closely followed by her breasts, her buttocks, her tights-tops, her underwear, all the ciphers of an old man's desires. It was all building up, it was all leading up. He spoke a little and serenely of the tedium of thirty-five years of marriage. He eased in his little cares, in among the forest of woes that was Mercy's. He planted herbaceous borders around her central arboretum.

They were so engrossed they didn't hear Frankie Chives sliding his way down the staircase, en route to his wheelchair parked in the alcove. Bump bump! Bump bump he went soundlessly, onto a thin cushion placed beneath his thighs. At each step the one-legged octogenarian raised himself a little, fell a little, continued his invalid's way down to the chair that would lead him on to the Great What Do They Call It?

'Pack up your troubles,' he sang in a sweet, deranged whisper, *'as you're doin' the Lambeth Walk.'*

He dragged himself the yard from the staircase bottom to his pair of crutches. Then quieter than an assassin he made it to the chariot that was not of fire. He had a box of matches which he was sorely tempted to strike and use to ignite this place where they had no respect for Scott nor for marriage. He held one in his hand, ready to strike. Then he heard shufflings and groans from inside the boss's door and gathered that *Gow-ells* and *Mer-ci-a* were either gum-kissing or doing some unspeakable magical hocus-pocus.

Frankie's contempt was utter. He tossed away the matches and primed his fists about his wheelchair. He pushed through the swingdoors and tasted the summer night. Up above Orion. In his left pocket *Ivanhoe.* In his right pocket *Redgauntlet.* Out there somewhere the Black Country. He started his chariot rolling, then set off with infinite care.

Master of Ceremonies

My grandfather enjoyed putting enormous fear into women...
Thus as early as I can remember my gentle old grandmother shook with nerves, like some wired electrical contraption. And her daughter, my mother, normally the one so fearless, one might say the bold fighter outside of her father's house, was also harshly cut to size by this irascible old man.

Even so it was untrue to say that he was cruel to all women and gentle with all men. Rather, any man whom he considered womanish - that is, in his terms, talkative, gossipy, nervous, without any centre of gravity - he also endeavoured to bully and mock. His nephew Sid being a good example, one of the men whose conversation my grandfather would punctuate with noisy spittings into the fire, whose opinions he would openly scoff at, whose exaggerations which nervous old Sid used to manufacture to impress us all, he would greet with a leer of fine contempt. Perhaps others felt the same way as my grandfather with regard to the jabberings of Sid. Certainly many of them, including nervous women, would treat him rather brusquely.

The old man never bullied me, nor attacked my own father. We were both very quiet, very shy, and it was obvious he respected us for that. Confident women too, ones so self-contained they made even him uneasy, he would leave well alone with his tongue. He was kind to small children, respectful to quiet men, hardworking, vain, Labour to the bone, compendiously bitter, prodigious of memory and story. He lived in the changeless past like others live in a vacuum of motion or talk. At home he liked to sit pensive and rock himself in the armchair, his personal armchair, planted there for at least one or two millennia so it seemed. From time to time his voice would rise up for a story and the household would turn its ears to the unchallenged master of ceremonies.

My grandmother and mother would listen because they were afraid to do anything else. I listened because I was a child and I was gripped by his brilliant tales. My father either attended or read away quietly in a corner. Most often I was the only really attentive audience, for who can be attentive when she or he is panicking? Thus he would turn to me the nine-year-old and focus his art upon me. One good listener being worth a thousand compliant faces of course. We became that age old partnership, the story-teller and his single-minded solitary listener.

My grandparents' house was a small, sad, terraced two-up, two-down, with no bathroom and no inside toilet. At the fronts it faced a parallel row of terraces and along the backs it had shabby allotments and the enormous aged gasworks. The smell of that gas I loved, it salted my nose, it salted the whole town and particularly its poorest end which was congregated there, in rows and rows of terraces identical to this one. From their back window you beheld the yard, roughly cobbled and walled in high on either side, blocked in at the front where the tall, painted gate was the towering means of exit. Out into the yard I would go if I needed fresh air or to urinate. I would enter the outside toilet, a small, narrow affair with the usual wind, stone and faecal smell, and leaving the door on the latch, would proceed to pee across the lettering that said *Shanks Twyford,* trying each time to follow the sequence of the letters and then starting again if I erred in my urinary progress. I never sat and squatted in that lavatory as I had a fear of being somehow locked inside in that eerie darkness. Besides, sometimes when I was in there, the neighbours would start their terrible show and that would be enough to get me skedaddling back into the house again and safety.

'There it goes again,' grumbled my grandfather stonily as I returned. 'That crazy idiot upsetting that laal lass. And this goes on from morning till night every single day...'

My mother looked deeply pitying. I felt much afraid. My father went on reading. My grandmother went on shaking. The bitch dog Lassie continued quaking in skinny sympathy. She was a little Lakeland terrier, already in her teens, safe with my grandmother and aware of the two faces of her master. He predictably would love her and terrorise her by turn.

38

'Will you hark at that racket?' he asked my mother with a poisoned face. 'If I was that bairn I'm bloody sure I'd blare twice as hard if I had to endure that damn soft bawlin'.'

Through the walls and also from the outside, over the wall of the yard, we could hear the neighbour playing his piano to accompany what sounded like opera or something as remarkable issuing from his lips. He was not playing and singing for his own entertainment but because his teenage daughter was weeping. His daughter was fifteen years old but was unable to sit upright or do anything but lie and most times cry. After the age of twelve months her body had ceased to grow and all the growth had continued in her head. Thus she had an enormous head and a tiny little body, hydrocephalic or macrocephalic, I believe, being the medical diagnosis.

'He says that it sometimes cheers her up,' remarked my grandmother pacifically. 'He says sometimes the singing stops the kiddie crying.'

'Pah,' snorted her husband quickly. 'There's many a time that laal lass is quiet, asleep or daydreamin' mebbe. And then that clown starts his mad caterwaulin' and the poor little beggar sets off yawlin' and bawlin'...'

My mother remarked with that melting, tender voice: 'It's such a shame. It's such a cross for that poor little girl.'

My grandmother, nodded, shook and agreed. She was shaking in the armchair that was placed against the window facing the yard. Her husband in his rocker was seated stiffly opposite, adjacent to the roaring coal fire. To his right was the table and round that were my parents and myself. I always sat the very nearest to my grandfather, like some shield, and my father always sat most remote as he went on with his quiet reading. The little bitch Lassie meanwhile was propped on my grandmother's pinny, as bright as a little sparrow and with that toothy grin little terriers often have in their senility.

'And she has such a pretty face,' said grandmother gently. 'It's an enormous one and yet it's such a bonny face that little creature has...'

'The poor little beggar,' repeated my mother, her eyes

glistening with strong compassion.

There were a few seconds respite. Grandfather's railway clock ticked away with its steady, sombre sound. The fire hissed and laughed in the old, black-painted grate. The aria singing bellowed on like pure insanity. Was the father weeping too as he sang for his miserable daughter? She never seemed to gain any relief at all from her keening and crying, sobbing and moaning, that wafted through the thin, old walls.

'I think,' said my grandfather with provocation, 'that that bairn should never have been allowed to live.'

There was the slightest, tensest pause. My mother kept quiet but my grandmother, who was indeed capable of rebellion and even quaking annoyance from time to time, muttered with impatience.

'*You* can't say that. Don't be wicked! Wisht with you, man!'

Everything in the room, even the wall-clock tautened. For we had been through this sequence many times. Grandfather was quite unmoved by the righteousness of my grandmother's tone. She had had religion and a lay-preacher father. He had always taken as much of that business, of religion, as he wanted. No more than a sneering trifle.

'It's plain fact,' he persisted, at first only loudly self-defensive. 'What joy does that poor laal bugger have, lyin' on her back all her damn days? What sort of a dog's life is yon, woman?'

'*You* cannot say,' my grandmother retorted, her shakes suddenly changing into the simple flush and movement of human emotion. Just then it was plain that her shakes were only her bottled-up heart, nothing more. Even I, a child, could see as much as that.

'What the deuce,' she went on, 'you can't be lettin' babies die, just because they're not a hundred per cent. There's no sense in that, that's wicked, foolish talk is that...'

'Oh?' he scoffed violently. 'You know where wickedness is, my lass? Wickedness is in lettin' that kid lie there year after year with a halfwit like that driving it crackers. That's what I call cruelty. And I'll say it again, they should just have let the poor thing die when they saw it was going to be like the monster it is. The doctors should just have let that bloody kiddie die!'

'But,' my grandmother protested with a red and passionate face, her shakes again suddenly transformed into the vibrations of her temper and her faith, 'the baby didn't start to go queer until it was twelve months. You can't go and kill a twelve-month-old baby even if you're ready to kill one that's just been born. Don't talk so damn wicked, man!'

She sat upright, her neck muscles were juddering, her head and trunk vibrant with the taste of her convictions. I admired her for once instead of feeling only pity for her. All the same there was something faintly comic in the set of her jaw and it was this which her husband proceeded at once to seize on.

'Look there!' he addressed us all sneeringly. 'The missus gettin' in a lather and bawlin' at the rest of us!'

'No,' my grandmother yelped sharply and shamefacedly. 'No I am not!'

'Oh but you are, my lass,' he taunted heartlessly. 'Great red face, neck shaking, hands going all over the shop. Look there, son, at your grandmother!' he added, as he looked to me for supportive mockery.

My grandmother hid her head. My mother attempted to change the subject and remarked in a rush on the volume of people up in the town centre. My father had hastily resumed his book. I was simply watching it all, helpless and riveted.

'And now she's datherin',' the old man went on victoriously. 'Just look at her shakin' away! Shakin' and shakin' like a bumble bee or a bit of grass! What is it then! Is it your *nerves?* Is it your nerves makin' you shake, my lass? I tell you, I wouldn't let *myself* shake like that! Would I hell! I'd pull myself together and stop myself. What - you're a nervous wreck you are, missus. You and the dog together both shakin' like a pair of bloody tambourines...'

He went on as cruelly as this for some time. At last my grandmother started to weep, and then attempted to hold and retract her tears. Finally she darted into the back kitchen and called from there with a shaky, anxious voice, to ask us if we'd all like a cup of tea and a bite to eat. My mother dashed through supposedly to give her a hand, but I could hear her whispering in a thick and protective voice, to ignore what her father had said. Just ignore him was her solemn advice.

But already the tormentor had resumed another tale and with me his listener he went on to exploit his gift of perfect recall.

Tea had commenced. Darkness was falling already, on a warmish evening at the tail end of April. My grandfather rose midway through the tea and switched on his massive old valve radio. Laboriously he fiddled through wavebands and volume controls until he had us all listening to *The Archers*. The radio as ever took a minute or so to warm up. It was like an animal, as big as a little old goat perhaps, and the many knobs on the front gave it a face and a personality of its own. Valve radios, surely they have a power and a magic second to none. That boom, crackle, inner world of the sound, that cave and echo wonder of it all. *The Archers* actually bored me to tears but just the resonant, foggy roar of the machine itself was enough to make my guts as warm and secure as an infant's.

Walter Gabriel made entrance and my grandfather laughed and chuckled away. He and my grandmother listened to the programme every evening and as my mother wistfully remarked were half-convinced that the Archers were real people living in a real village and having their dramas at a regular time of the day, just as we chose to eavesdrop on them.

Immediately it finished the old man went and sharply switched it off. Then he slowly returned to the rocker while my mother and grandmother gratefully rushed to the pots and pans. My father at once rose and offered his help but was craftily returned to the sitting room to keep the old man company. It was black dark outside but naturally no electric light went on until my grandfather allowed it. Instead we sat in the gloaming with that roaring fire from the grate, and he and my father lit up their first of many evening pipes. If my father happened to be near enough the fire then he was deviously able to keep on his reading; if not he was forced to be a nodding listener too. But eventually my grandfather would realise the strain on my father's eyes and gently rise to put on the light. Left to their own routine he and his wife often sat for hour after remarkable hour in the firelit darkness until they wended off to bed at nine or ten.

In the gloaming the stories were even better. My grandfather interspersed them with prods at the fire and with the slow mechanics of his pipe. He would lean down from his rocker and poke with the bright new alloy poker Sid had brought him. Impurities in the coal might spark up and glow out green, blue, yellow and black. I gazed into the grate and saw the perfection of embers, incandescence. I listened to all that sissing and singing from the flames. My father would gaze like myself in a reverie at the fire. Much later I was to learn that certain primitive people made a god or a totem out of fire and it wasn't at all impossible to forecast as much just then.

And from time to time the old man's pipe would empty, so that he would take out his tobacco tin, a shiny, polished, circular bewitching tin much more like an empty watchcase than a tobacco-pouch. He would snap it open and pull out his twist tobacco, a material which looks like nothing so much as dried dog shit. Or like a dark brown rope which needs to be cut and rubbed before it can be pressed into the mouth of the pipe. Then the old man had to ceremoniously light it. He had no taste for matches, particularly in the sacred time of evening gloaming. If the light was on I could see the colours of the spills which he poked down into the blasting fire. He had a box at his feet which contained spills of all vivid colours; blue, green, red and yellow. He would pull one out and hold it slowly in the singing flames. Bent down to the grate for this, the elaborate lighting would be done in a leisurely, poetic, meditative way. Then he would cast the remnant into the fire, return to his private throne and his latest, strangest, memory-perfect recollection.

My grandfather had no time for matches though to be sure he needed at least one to light the fire in the morning, just as my grandmother needed some in her shaky hands for the gas cooker in the tiny, primitive kitchen she kept. Separate, greatly elevated from these were my grandfather's *special* matches and these were something to which one might devote a whole treatise, had one the poetry and the skill to tease out their mysterious significance as kernel memories. Those special matches were a souvenir someone had fetched him from a Morecambe tobacconist's about a decade earlier. They were in effect like match versions of his spills, for they were all the colours of the rainbow too, those match heads where the phosphorus was dyed red, yellow, blue, green and even some chalk-coloured whites were to be found. All the colours were jammed together in what was a cylinder-shaped box with a plastic, transparent top. The reds were together, the blues together, the yellows together, and they were all framed within an oval top which made them appear like a set of lustrous, beautifully-coloured families. Of course, the box was never opened. The matches were never used. They stayed pristine, unstruck, perfect and blindingly coloured.

I have never ever seen colours like the colours of those matches. They shone like stars or like angels. They were so beautiful they could hypnotise me for minutes at a time. I wanted to eat them, swallow them, inhale them, partake of them, enjoy and imbibe and impress on myself their lustre and other-worldly radiance...

My grandmother saw me looking at those matches and commented tenderly on how rapt I seemed. My grandfather looked at them and then me proudly and unselfishly. My grandmother asked me if I wasn't going to put the calendar right for her today, as I had every other time I came visiting. I rose shyly and stepped self-consciously as I made over to the sideboard to do the job that was mine.

It was a little brass holder with a moulded horse emblem on the top. Inside the holder went three different sizes of card. At the front of the holder went the smallest proclaiming the weekday, Tuesday. Behind it the lesser giving the number of the month, the twenty-seventh. After that, the particular month, which was April. It was a laborious, endless business getting it all to rights, particularly when as now the calendar hadn't been put right for a month or so. That cheap little ornament-calendar had the innocent grace of all familiar, simple things. Its smallness, its friendly brass mimicry of a horse. I felt my grandparents' eyes trained upon me as I did my job and I performed it with a sense of duty and a sense of untold, unexplainable necessity. As if I was marking time for them always.

The old man had been retired for over a dozen years, but he maintained a part-time job. He was out working in some shopkeeper's greenhouses for thirty or more hours a week and in 1961 was being paid two pounds ten-and-sixpence for this. His relatives talked of the exploitation involved but my grandfather was coolly indifferent to anything but the work itself. He liked to be busy and would have been even harsher if left to his memories and nothing besides. In any case, what use was an abundance of money to such as *him?*

Those hours he was working were the ones where my grandmother was left to bathe her broken nerves. She went out and shopped, took Lassie out down by the back of the gasworks, sat on her own in the house and shook and cooked and waited. She lived in a permanent melancholy apprehension that was excited and maintained by her husband, Jackie Spade. Her pleasures were her relatives, her packets of sweets, her daily listen to *The Archers* and presumably her sleep. The doctor gave her tablets but they made no real difference to her terrors. If the doctor had had any sense of metaphor he might have given the pills to my grandfather instead. As it was my grandfather would have as soon approached a doctor as approach a clergyman. He thought of medicine and the ill as feeble and despicable. My grandmother, left to her own devices, used to perform a soothing nervous tic with her hands. She would cause them to revolve round and round each other just as if carding some imaginary wool. There remained, nonetheless, the problem of her neck; nothing that she knew of could stop the bouncings and twitchings of that agile limb.

Except for one remarkable thing. A friend of a friend of the man for whom my grandfather did his part-time job, one day gave my grandfather a television. We couldn't think why the old man should have accepted such a gift seeing that he had long made plain his hatred for that invention and seeing that he was as resistant to charity as he was to the pills of doctors. Later we learnt that he had perhaps parted with some cash, or it might have been so many weeks wages given in part-payment via his employer. However, economics aside, his authority had to find some way of addressing itself to the invasion of this impudent-faced intruder.

His relationship with the television was from the start a dubious one. His wife naturally fell in love with it from the very first half hour. She also soon found the televisual equivalent of *The Archers* in terms of that novel, realistic series called *Coronation Street* and another less demanding show called *Yorkie,* starring Wilfred Pickles, was soon to draw her to the screen like a love-starved addict.

My grandfather noticed this particular fascination. He noticed several things as he observed his wife now so fascinated with something new that effectively he, Jack Spade, had taken a rear seat in the audience. This new machine had much more power to it than the ageing, weary old radio. The only radio programme his wife showed any passion for was *The Archers* but with the television it seemed she would have gawped at anything given the chance. Jack Spade commented on that with some sarcasm and some disdain. He used the word 'brainwashed' and watched with pleasure as she started and flushed. She strove to deny the addiction but in his own cruel way he was right. She knew he was right and the tears welled up in her cornflower-blue, meek eyes. Thus she always watched in panicking doubt her *Coronation Street* and said little prayers all the time that she watched it. Impermanence, anxious impermanence, was always a part of her despicable addiction.

To start with my grandfather kept the television down below the wireless and covered with a cloth, just as if it was a budgerigar taking a permanent night's rest. The radio sat on top of the table and in order for the TV to be switched on, the two

46

must change places and thereby the radio be humiliated and demoted. Was it that the old man was just sentimental and wished not to see the old replaced by the new? After all, he could not exactly help himself from being just as glued to *Coronation Street,* especially if he thought that no one was looking at his line of gaze...

If his wife wished to watch any other programme she had to ask him to put the TV up there for her. She would no more have switched it on herself than have stolen his personal rocking chair. And for those first few weeks it suited him to make much heavy weather of it all and to do the replacement and the switching on with something of an effort and a show of generosity. He carried it out with painstaking resistance. He lingered long over the performance in order to enjoy her lasting apprehension.

Weeks passed and my grandfather became most unnerved. His wife's enjoyment of *Coronation Street* was so profound that when it was on it left him feeling old and helpless and almost like an accessory to the room. To his room! All else aside it was impossible for him just to ruminate and daydream with that infernal blaring. It dominated the room, overwhelmed the atmosphere in a way that the radio could never hope to do. It dominated his wife, where formerly he had dominated his wife. There was an irritating competition there. There had to be a stop put somewhere.

One night my grandmother made her very last request for him to put on his television. It was seven twenty-five and it was a Monday. Last Wednesday had been a real cliff-hanger where Ena Sharples had been left for dead, Jack, she mumbled to the old man very frightenedly. Her hands dathered as usual, her neck twitched and begged for some kind of attention and tenderness, even if it only be in other folks' lives on that magical ridiculous seventeen-inch screen.

'No,' he refused expressionlessly, rocking in his rocker, fingering his dark brown twist tobacco.

'Please!' she begged, not knowing whether to be relieved or to weep now that the blow had fallen.

47

'No,' he repeated calmly, and then added for good measure, 'You're getting brainwashed by that thing, my lass! It's taking you over. It's making you soft! You're sat there like a cow with your nose an inch from that screen and it's the only thing that gives you any interest in life. You should give yourself a shake! You should be ashamed of yourself! Isn't it a fact that it's brainwashing you that blasted telly?'

'No,' she wept, just as Lassie squatted on her haunches and begged for a look from her double.

'I think so,' he said, almost conversationally.

'Please,' she implored, her shakes letting loose like ten cannons.

'No,' he said, suddenly happily, 'and that's final. I said no and I meant it, lass! And tomorrow I'm giving it back to that feller, that television. I hate it! It rules everything. What, all our folks, all our relatives and their bairns, do nowt but watch that bloody thing. All day, all night, like machines. They're mad! They want their heads looked! I'm damned if I'm gonna be ruled by a thing like yon from mornin' till night...'

Until, two years later, he was seventy-eight. In my mother's opinion her parents were getting far too old to fend for themselves so she scoured about for a house close to ours, so that she could minister as a daughter should. Soon she had acquired a tiny cottage that was hardly ten yards from our own. The old man made enough protests but eventually agreed to the move. His wife was delighted of course... for not only would she have an escape from her husband, she would also have access to a nineteen-inch television.

I was growing up just as they were growing very old. My secondary schooling corresponded to those last six years of my grandfather's life. My father had got him an allotment in the village and every day, rain, shine, wind, drought, the old, determined, stern and wrinkled man pedalled his two miles there and back. My grandmother sat with my mother through much of the day and twice a week for all those years she would come across to watch her *Coronation Street*. She must have watched at least six hundred episodes before she died. She had gained that much freedom, that three hundred hours, for not even Jack Spade would have presumed to bar the door against her evening exits.

In 1968, at just turned eighteen, I won myself a place at one of our ancient universities. The results came on a day when my parents were out shopping and there was no one with whom I might share my ecstatic news. I, who hardly went near my grandparents from one year to the next, I suddenly remembered two people to whom I could relate my present glories. I scuttered off those ten yards to inform them of the prowess of their magical grandson. I was elated with pride and vanity and pleasure. I had worked like a single-minded maniac to get my prize and now I was basking like a pampered lapdog.

My grandmother was tickled to the skies. She took out a dusty bottle of sherry, her hands quaking as she poured, and drank to my success. My grandfather sat in his rocker, nodding himself backwards and forwards and digesting the news with curiosity. He shook his head up and down with that emphasis of old and repeated the syllables of that famous university town.

'Very good,' he said with solemn scrutiny. 'Well, well. That's done it and make no mistake.'

My grandmother echoed the magical syllables too. That city to her, to him, to me also in my provincial fantasies, was half way between Eldorado and Olympus. Getting into *that* university was tantamount to having won through the labours of an epic hero. I saw the pride on their faces and knew now why it meant so very much to me that victory. One's own pride was only one's pride for others, a means of glowing before others who could perhaps not really see what was there at one's roots.

'Here's to you,' said my quaking grandmother, her neck going to left and right as she spoke, adding as she toasted how proud and pleased my two parents would be.

'Oh aye,' said my grandfather with proprietorial wisdom, as if it was only he had ever really understood me and my ways. And then, '*I* knew how brainy this feller was. I knew all along about this feller. What, I can mind how sharp he was as a bairn.

I could have telled you all how well this lad would do in time...'

He nodded backward and forward in his chair and sucked away wisely at his pipe.

'But you know,' he said obscurely, 'you should rest your brains, lad, sometimes. Too much bookwork can be a bad thing for you. You should relax your brains now and again.'

My heart stabbed painfully. *What* was it he saw? Anything, nothing, the roots of my ambition? And where would the memory of such as Jackie Spade fit within the portals of that church-university, that town for the elect, the chosen, the blessed ones?

'This lad'll end up one of the gentry,' concluded my grandfather. 'This lad'll end up among the toffs. And good for him! You go out there son and beat the bloody lot of them, toffs and all!'

He was dead about six months later. In the early winter of 1969 he found himself too weak to cycle down to the allotments. For two, perhaps three months, he was there struggling with the final blows, upstairs in his bed, tossing and turning and forgiving no one in his steady way. He begged for no contrition, no unction, no attentions. He wanted no nursing. He told the nurses to let him die, without self-pity or dramatising, and he meant it. Because, of course, in the last few weeks it was bed-washing, rubber rings and all that monstrous palaver. And along with that his mind would take him for walks all over the past. He who had lived in the past in word now lived in the past in thought and substance. He believed himself to be back down the pits (where he had worked before the railways) and he cursed the unyielding nature of the coal and the earth and I was told he swore obscenely as he did so.

They told me to go and see him and I would not. My grandmother asked, my mother asked, my father suggested it but I would not go and see him. Besides, as my grandfather had shrewdly seen, I just hadn't the time to bless myself these days. I still had A levels to sit and as everyone knows those things are closer to God than are grandfathers. Like a well-oiled machine I studied, fretted, keened and quietly suffered. Those who can guess what I am talking about will know what I am talking about. I never paid him his last respects. I refused to go and see him on his death bed. I stayed where I was and I studied.

When he died it turned out that he had left me, me uniquely of his many grandchildren, one of his special Victorian sovereigns. My grandmother handed me that along with the little horse emblem calendar, the unstruck perfect matches, the look of a far-away widow.

She wept long after the death of her tormentor. She lived another nine months was all. We could judge how affected she was by his absence inasmuch as she used to fall asleep watching her *Coronation Street* where before she was as alert as her little bitch Lassie had long ago been.

She spent all her time sleeping, falling asleep, thinking about doing so... and thinking perhaps of all the years she had endured under Jackie - the emphatic - Spade. People said it was his nagging must have kept her alive. Others that it was that which had left her so exhausted when she was only seventy-five. By early 1970 she was in bed and breathless and in three weeks she was dead.

I had felt nothing when he died and I felt nothing again when his wife went. By then I was in the ancient city which left me for some reason no time to feel sorrow nor loss nor anything whatever. I remember trying to cry over the death of my gentle, long-haired grandmother, she who would have been as near to a blamelessness of character as anyone. Nothing would come. Not even a single drop could be squeezed.

Until all of ten years after. I was lying awake in a distant Midlands township, in a town that my grandfather would have hated. It was a town that had no taste, smell, vigour, past, future. It had two dozen supermarkets, DIY shops, traffic islands, multi-storey car parks, hypermarkets, new estates, prosperity - in a word fuckall. My wife and I were living on an estate of semis where the neighbours were to say the least far less vigorous than the cadavers who dwelt in the adjacent cemetery. In fact the cemetery was the only beautiful thing in

51

that Midlands town. It had a few weeds, a look of age, an air of being lived in as it were.

I saw his matches in the gloaming, as I lay awake, thinking just as he always did of the past. I saw the colours of his *special* matches in their brightness, their beauty, their glory. The memory had come because of first simply thinking of Cumberland. Rootless at home, rootless in exile, it was all one and the same was it not? Little terriers, little bitch terriers cracking stones between their teeth in grey and smoky backyards. Old men bullying old women. Ambitious children trying to win their way from the backyards of the future. All those handsome, televisual dreams of Getting On and Doing Very Well At All Costs.

And then the floodgates opened up. All at once the colours of the matches turned into smell and turned into grief. I could smell them, him, her, Lassie and her small tin box, that house, that fire, the gas works, the cream cakes bought by my mother. I could see it all like gold and would have sold my body and soul just to have smelt it all for good.

The Señor and the Celtic Cross

One way of describing his remarkable progress would be to say that he moved from a big island to a small island to a very tiny one. Then when he reached the very tiny one he went out to its furthest end and stood on a solitary rock five feet out in the bright green Atlantic sea. There he was at a fourth stage of remoteness and felt himself almost securely positioned as a result.

This young man of twenty-four, who gave his surname as Stone, attained a fourth stage of subordination and in doing so he found himself exploring a fourth layer of private weakness. Because on his journey from the large island to the rock in the sea off the tiny island, he encountered a man who disturbed him, a sign which disturbed him, and a woman who took his breath away. Finally the woman departed, leaving Stone feeling for her with all his heart and soul, and the interesting thing is that before this final adventure he was well-nigh convinced he possessed neither heart nor soul nor any memory of them.

It would be forgivable to fabricate that Stone had just escaped from prison, it would make his desperation plainer. The stranger he met, who gave his name as Dukes, saw this situation clearly. Dukes was a confident dabbler in the occult, in the somewhat democratic manner in which all sorts of eccentrics these days are confessedly 'into' Tarot, or are exponents of the Qabbala, or perhaps claim to have analysed and made full sense of the Revelations of St John of Patmos. Dukes was also sexually attracted to Stone - or Stone had been born yesterday if Dukes was not. Dukes had terribly vulnerable eyes which when he was hurt would fade over and grow misted with an affecting desolation. It takes a haunted one to spot another haunted one, thought Stone, when Dukes got to the significant point of elucidating the desperation of Stone in terms of the fig-leaves of the occult.

Dukes was probably forty-four, certainly no more than forty-six. How on earth does one know these things? He was short-haired, brown as a hazel nut, trim and remarkably upright of gait, almost as if he were an Indian village lady walking to the well with a water pitcher. He wore a dark, dowdy anorak in the Hebridean rain, a garment that was attractive in its spare austerity. His whole life was a tribute to the spirit of austerity. It was to be a week before he disclosed his spiritual side to Stone but if Stone had been any wiser than he was he would have forecast as much by that interesting devotion to simplicity in Dukes.

Stone had left his abode for a month, four and a half weeks, and was on a directionless pilgrimage. He was also vacant, not in the pejorative sense but simply empty as a water pitcher. He took route and moved north from what the Gaelic-speakers call *Sasainn*. Then he took a second route from that town which they likewise name *Glaschu*. He came to the noisy, colourful seaport with his bag and his small green tent, modelled after the slope and structure of a gypsy's and hence called a tinker-tent. The lively port had been christened originally *an-t-Oban*. He spent one night camping opposite the nearby isle of Kerrera. There were midges by the million but the weather was so warm and the view so comforting that he paid little attention to his constant scratching. It was a species of farm he was camped upon and the old farmer's four ancient and reckless sheepdogs raced about woofing and tumbling each other. There was a tin-sheeting roof next to Stone's tinker-tent and those mad sheepdogs raced round and round on that rusting tin, making such a clatter that Stone's heart reached up with joy. For what could be more entertaining than to experience the anarchy of humble beasts engaged in the unsayable ecstasy of incalculable pleasure?

The next day he took the ferry over to, so to speak, *Muile*. On his path to the jetty he observed the irises and fuchsias which stood like wayside shrines. They breathed, glistened and smiled in the drowsy sweat heat of late June. It was very hot. Heat is a drug that, as a rule, costs nothing. Stone went up on the ferry and mingled with the passengers on deck. He saw two very attractive young women, four, six, about a dozen handsome young women. One of them took his breath away, but do not be misled into thinking this is the same woman who really was to take his breath away. Yet she induced in him real breathlessness and his heart lurched at the sight of such a beauty. This girl (later she will appear under the name of Kate) had a smoothly-tanned face and that kind of glistening, fading liquidity of eye which arouses all tenderness in the heart of a tender man. She had an oval face. But then again boiled eggs are oval. To be precise, she had a face like a slim egg of a delicate bird. Her hair was fair beyond all fairness. She made Stone's heart bleed with desire, with a keening desire that feels like an impenitent ache. She was in conversation with a young man who was a dupe, a kind-hearted young dupe, and another woman, later to appear as Jane, who would have been a fit companion for the dupe had she taken to his pleasant, companionable ways. He was shy and nervous, blond-locked and stammering, and had just happened to fall into conversation with this beautiful woman who was the friend and travel partner of the woman called Jane.

Bonny Kate laughed with full knowledge of her power, upon the sunny deck of that steamer to *Muile*. She played with the dupe not cruelly, but capably. She knew at once how much his heart beat violently for her. Stone picked up the accents of the lively trio and discerned that they were good ones. It was a well-spoken trio. Kate's charm was easy and not the charm that appealed to Stone yet he wanted her as others want the dawn or the drug.

Two or three days passed on the isle *of Muile* - for the man with his bright green tinker-tent. The weather stayed hot and the surroundings he found for himself were very strong. He parked his home only a few yards from the narrow road with its passing places and its small amount of traffic. To his right was the bay, a matter of a dozen yards down onto wrack-covered rocks and then the stony strand. The heat was baking and the sea was almost warm. Despite self-admonition, he kept his eyes peeled for the passage of those two women...

Happier he was though to want no one and nothing. The rich weather helped him in this and he was also pleased to sit reading from hour to hour. He was glad to just squat and respire like an insect in the sun. The bay was broad and bright blue and made him feel expansive as it was itself. Across on the other side, on the mainland, were the hills and cottages of *Ard-na-murchan*. Like a sleepwalker a ferry would glide to and from *an-t-Oban* every hour. People would wave at his tent from their cars, something about its size and its simple appearance seemed to impress them. Even solitary Stone seemed to strike them as worthy of a greeting this way.

Then one day it rained...

It gave itself up to downpour. The Gaelic-speakers know plenty about rain and make it the rhythm of their poetry. Stone was confined to his tinker dwelling where he sat in his solitude with only books for company. He also had food, chocolate, cigarettes, money, security for a month or so. After that he had his abode in *Sasainn* (to adopt a fresh perspective) and what? Plans to roam the earth, to create a stir? All was in flux, just as for instance the Buddha had described it. But why did Stone find religion *so* embarrassing? Because he was like the rest of his contemporaries? Alone in his tent in the teeming rain no one knew anything of any of these meagre reflections of course. He might just as well have been invisible. It goes without saying that many a time Stone, like many a loner before him, experienced himself as invisible, unreachable, indefinable and beyond the laws of nature.

Soon the steam and the damp midges in his tent became unbearable. He donned his waterproofs and left the tent to take a breath of air. Still it teemed and Stone felt disconsolately that perhaps it might rain for the rest of his life. What had been glistening blue sea and yellow-black beatified rock only yesterday was just grey and wet and inconsequence today. God had run from this place and left a void of damp and drear.

Then from the corner of his eye came a rapid signal. There a hundred yards before him, parading down the narrow island road, came a short, thin, graceful figure muffled in a dark, plain protective garment. Even his hood was tied up to the nose. There was no excess, no extra to his dripping, confident appearance. This was Dukes on his way to the public house to fill his little water carrier. Dukes the one who stopped and made a friendly, authoritative hello. Dukes who seemed to know his own mind, to speak as if appointed, to halt as if commanded, to relish in a modest way the presence of his own presence. At once he attracted and repelled Stone. For he walked so straight, so stiffly straight and perpendicular.

They made affable, attractive conversation. Dukes had a warm wit, a Lowland wit, that relished exaggeration, belittling, irony. Stone came from far enough north in... *Sasainn*... to appreciate the flavour of Dukes' banter. They were racially close enough to taste each other's sympathies in wit. One spoke, the other parried, one jested, the other laughed.

Dukes' story was astonishing. He related it with pride, authority, yet modesty, and yet the pride informed the modesty. This man in his forties was *walking* the whole length of the Scottish coastline. He had been on the road for two months already, striding up from Galloway, across to the east, up around Banff, Sutherland, Ross, down through Moray, down to Argyll and now onto the isles. A small amount of hitch-hiking the likes of tractors, the occasional ferry across a narrow waterway, living not by shops and cash but by hand and mouth, by hunting and fishing like some Neanderthal man. Even his tent was just a sheet of gardening plastic suspended over two handy sticks...

Out of one of his pockets he pulled a large, ugly catapult, which he explained he used for slaying rabbits. From another pocket came a small, green-coloured handline for angling his fish. He described how he pilfered farmers' fields for potatoes and other trifling things. Then he pointed proudly to thick bracken reaching up the hillock that was half a mile off in the mist.

'My tent's in that lot,' he murmured to Stone. 'Buried away.

I like my seclusion you see. I value my seclusion more than almost anything. Do you not yourself, son?'

This was said with an open uncomplicated humour. The elder man asked Stone nothing about himself during that half hour conversation in the rain. Yet Dukes did not appear to hide anything. He seemed to be content and unhurried, glad of his solitude, strong in himself. He seemed to be the opposite of Stone who was moody, impatient, restless, always wondering what lay next and the next after that. Dukes took Stone in hand as a matter of course. He exercised power and authority in a wholly invisible way. He invited him to go along to the nearby hotel-cum-public house that evening. The rain teemed down before Stone's doubtful eyes, yet the friendliness and good nature of this elder man, seemed a thing both strong and worth the gamble.

Soon Dukes became a constant irritating contour of Stone's landscape. The day following that first meeting was as hot as the days that went before it. A second hot spell had set in. Ripe hot weather always works steady miracles. Everyone feels his skin opening up, the bounty of the elements, the richness of sensual life to be found in the air itself, but richest of all in forests, by roadsides, down by the weed-infested strand. Everything ticks in the heat, like a lazy old bomb, a harmless self-annihilation, a wished-for nothingness. And Dukes became gradually mysteriously inseparable from Stone, much as Stone attempted to prise himself apart...

In the public house lo and behold beautiful Kate and less beautiful Jane were working as barmaids and general hotel servants. This raised Stone's expectations to sheer absurdity. Bold Dukes had a way of talking to anyone as easily and commandingly as if he were the whole world's father. He chatted generously to Kate who wrenched provocatively those pints of heavy behind the hotel bar, a holiday job before she went up to the university in England to study of all things European Philosophy. She was such a gentle-contoured, wispy-eyed young woman. By virtue of the way she addressed the world she was one who could only be addressed herself either seductively or teasingly - the latter being the fatherly manner adopted by wise old Dukes. Unfortunately the sight of her melting, darting eyes was like the Koh-i-Noor to young Stone who attempted to elaborate his attraction with a quiet and mendacious confidence. He talked to her with expanded lips and nostrils, tried philosophical matter as a superior gambit, with subtle communication of a special relationship, a prized potential which only ones like he and Kate were worthy of. Without putting it into words he intimated that he Stone and she Kate were, of all the hundred souls inside this public house, special and exotic and exquisite.

Dukes would regularly undo all of this, even though nothing specific had been uttered by Stone that could have been attacked as youthful arrogance. Whenever Stone was trying to alchemise subtle intimacy and induce desire by magical means in Kate, fatherly Dukes was always there by his elbow dropping a joke or introducing an aside that somehow brought everything down to banal, unmagical level. It was as if Dukes was against magic. Perhaps he wanted Stone to himself, perhaps it was as simple as that. Perhaps he was Stone's protector, saw something in Kate that made him wish to hold the young man off for his own protection.

Jane was dull. She had the face of a startled, chubby Alice. She had no aurora. She had blinking nervous eyes and a rush and gabble caught-in-the neck way of talking that reminded Stone of the anchors of class and origin. These little Hebridean islands were full of rich, well-born people from *Sasainn.* Kate and Jane came from large houses in places like Surrey and Kent, for which no Gaelic words exist, being as - to reverse all logic - herring and oatmeal have little currency in Godalming or in Chatham. She seemed to be simply a chaperone to Kate, subordinate, the dull metric balance that is often to be found beside magnetic and over-beautiful women. Stone felt with irritation that Dukes was an equivalent ballast in his own case; even though he was an interesting, commanding and powerful person, he was still a barrier to intimacy with smooth-faced

Kate.

Dukes guided and annexed Stone over the next few days. On the Sunday he took him handline fishing down by the old jetty, the one that was now disused but where in the old days the ferry from Lochaline had docked en route to Tobermory. All the while Stone was keening for Kate but in a quiet, concealed way. Dukes seemed to know as much but as they fished kept up his flow of cheerful, informative talk. He told of a detailed and curious diary he was writing of his travels around his country. He recounted a little of his rich past, described pungently the army and the National Service and the adventures he had had in foreign towns. Really his conversation was diverting by any standards, he was an intriguing man with an intriguing past. Why then was Stone only half listening and feeling importuned? He had had enough of Dukes' company but Dukes would not let him go. En route to the shops and the public house he always called by the young man's tent, dropped by as a close companion would. He seemed to have taken the meandering young man under his wing, as if he was a puny fledgling. Stone saw that Dukes in part saw through to Stone's marrow, that he had eyes which saw much. Also that Dukes was paradoxically blind to all sorts of things. Dukes dissimulated fatigue when he was bored, unlike baleful Stone. Dukes patronised the most unpromising, helpless souls, in fact spurned no one. He was human, he was kind, he showed charity. Stone shied away from pests. This much was evident enough in the company of the loose network of campers, cyclists, walkers who used the nearby hotel as their meeting ground. He even befriended the young dupe, did Dukes, even was kind to the stuttering young toff who wormishly surrendered his little car to Kate and Jane on their afternoons off from hotel work. The dupe acted chauffeur for them around the isle of *Muile* every afternoon.

Yet as they fished Dukes soon perceived Stone's distraction and preoccupation. He decided anxiously to push the harder with his anecdotes and humour. He told stronger adventures, curiouser items of country lore and animal sightings discovered by the solitary traveller. He became a little desperate. The sight of the younger man's indifference to his tales at one stage seemed to cut him to the bone. Stone saw his face colour over with the grey hue of neglect, of year long sorrows. He saw the sorrowing side of Dukes. It was the flat grief of missing affections. What was that in essence?

Dukes was relating the story of his snake bite, one he had suffered in Spain when hiking there one year. How he had been utterly alone and had had to use his own penknife to slice himself and suck out the venom before hobbling in agony to the nearest town and doctor. A matter of life against...

'Weren't you afraid of dying?' asked Stone, at last showing interest.

'No,' said Dukes, more brightly, yet scornful of the question. 'Not of *that* yan.'

'What do you mean?'

'Yon death. Not of yon.'

He spoke of it like some ludicrous affliction.

'Well I for one am afraid of dying,' admitted Stone, keen at last to pursue the discussion.

But Dukes was talking of something else by this stage. He had all the habits of the monologuist. In fact he was resorting to vacuous patter. He was mumbling nervously about the fish being ready to bite here any minute now. So far, after three hours, neither of them had caught a thing...

That evening there was a *ceilidh* in the village, and Stone hoped Dukes would not attend it. But Dukes did, he called punctually for Stone at his tent and accompanied him to the hotel and then to the Parish Rooms where the drinkless entertainment began about ten o'clock. There was nevertheless much drunkenness, for people carried bottles of whisky out of the hotel bar. During the evening the two men had chatted with the two young women and Stone had felt that with luck perhaps the four of them would end up partners at the *ceilidh*. He even perceived a courtly side to Dukes. He also perceived that the world might be curious about this friendship between two men twenty years apart. Did they think Dukes was his father, his lover or his guardian? He edged away from the other man and tried to capture Kate by daring proximity. She in turn flattered and fluttered but gave nothing away. She oscillated between the bar and their table for she was half on duty and half off it this evening. It was uncertain whether she was responding. It was uncertain and therefore unlikely but Stone could not see that. In any case he hoped, he hoped with all his might.

The two women had to absent themselves from the table for the last half hour before the *ceilidh*. Dukes had drunk a substantial amount of liquor and was grown more than a little maudlin. He spoke of Stone moving his tent to where his own lay, tucked away in the sheltering bracken. Did Stone see? In fact why use two tents when one was sufficient for both of them? Why not pool their resources? As plain as that. It was spoken in an open, uncompromising way and for all the obvious lubricity of such a suggestion there was no way Stone could voice aloud that he was being propositioned by this man. In fact he was, anyone neutral could have discerned as much, Stone himself was probably shrewder in these matters than most... and yet Dukes' moral authority - for that was what it was, that constant generous cheerfulness - did not allow him to impute purely selfish sexual desire.

Stone skirted the maudlin suggestion. He said that he liked his privacy. He was on firm ground there because it was Dukes' constant boast that he needed his own seclusion. That matter was dropped and without embarrassment on either side. Indeed Dukes gratefully perceived how the young man was unable to think ill of his suggestion, as if hypnotised by that something special that marked out Dukes among the rest of them here in the bar tonight.

The *ceilidh* came and the evening went. Before long Stone and his bodyguard were dancing with Kate and her chaperone. Young Stone had his hard breast against young Kate's and he was torn by true ecstasy, on fire with the drug of her sweetness. Such delight in him unnerved her, therefore she was obliged to mask her unnervedness. She danced with dozens that night in any case, a beauty such as hers being the target of the eyes of all greedy, immature young men on holiday here. Even dull Jane had more than her fair share of pursuers. Then Stone blinked twice, perhaps he went to the Gents for a minute or so, and when he returned the two women had *vanished* from the scene...

He was mad with frustration. Bitterness sucked at his veins. He danced with all and sundry after that, defiantly, ready to court and mount the ugliest hag on all of *Muile*. If Dukes came by he kept away from him, for Dukes saw him chewing his spleen and knew the reason why, and that angered Stone, for he was aware that Dukes realised how greedy he was for flesh, no matter what spirit, so to speak, went with what flesh. He was aware of his own stupidity and yet he was annoyed that such as Dukes should stand smugly distant and contemplate wisely that undisguised folly.

After the *ceilidh* the dancers stood around in the warm and moonlit night, much laughter and drunken good humour passed around the deserted roads and sleeping township in this quiet island. Dukes was in rich, unquashable spirits, and he was charitably pitying of Stone who was so obviously discontented with the results of his unfulfilled desires. It was a beautiful night and he seemed to be intimating that everything was here to please Stone's heart if he could only forget about the Kates of this world.

'Where is she?' asked Stone cravingly, desperately, a little drunk by now. 'I thought we would have *had* those two.'

'Eh?' said Dukes indulgently.

'Kate. I thought you and Jane had reached an agreement. I thought we all had. Where the hell did they go? Why the hell did they run off?'

Dukes only smiled, the answer being so obvious.

The next day Dukes attacked him. That is he cut him down to size with the hatchet of his studies. Which was wielded relatively gently for all it followed on the older man's sexual frustration and also the bitterness he must have swallowed at the indifference of Stone.

Dukes had dragged Stone into the little township that day.

Stone was rebellious at being press-ganged into companionship, and in any case all he could think about was the breast and the thighs and the loins of Kate the barmaid. This June heat made him feel like a swollen phallus and nothing else. He was sick with sex and here he was with a middle-aged homosexual bursting his insides for him. He wanted Kate, Dukes wanted him, Kate wanted no one, no one wanted Dukes. Such chains, such fecund linkages, such holy bindings...

They were in a café when Stone's unremitting absence finally ruffled Dukes into his attack. For he had been telling the Englishman about the suspected... albatross... he'd sighted that morning as he took his dawn swim in the bay of Salen.

'An albatross?' exclaimed Stone, snapping into life again.

'I'm sure it was,' enthused Dukes gratefully. 'It's just possible a bird like yon would be traversing these wee isles. You see...'

Then he went on vividly about birds, about his practice of rising at dawn, of doing a little Hatha Yoga, of tasting a solitude beyond solitudes. To no avail. There was slim, doubting, hungering Stone dreaming of blonde-haired women with heavy breasts and sweet behinds and bonny eyes. Dukes could see the teats and fannies in his eyes. Dukes' power was negligible therefore. All that he'd done, all that he knew, all these wonderful tales that were his and all for Stone's enjoyment and sharing - spurned!

'Listen - do you believe in any *occult* matters?' he suddenly challenged the daydreamer aggressively.

Stone started. Dukes clenched his palm. At last! He knew where things stood! He saw Stone panic at the prospect of some strange intelligence.

'What?' he mumbled with a visible quiver. 'No. Yes. No.'

The Lowlander laughed. Kindness was still the master. He looked at Stone like a loving father. To Stone's amazement he noticed incredible similarity between this man and his own father. They had the same chin, same smile, same thinness, identical gentle manners. Who then *was* this bloody Dukes?

'You sound doubtful.'

'Yes.'

'Why is that?'

'It's... oh it's easy to laugh at. Hocus-pocus. Hypo-chondriacs. Crackpots. People with axes to grind.'

Stone's voice was aggressively defensive. He resented that look of placid omniscience in the other's eyes.

'I read the future,' announced Dukes matter-of-factly.

Stone made no reply.

'I have testimonials,' he added, a little naively.

'You what?'

'I'm no charlatan. I've helped so many people.'

'Oh?' blushed Stone. 'What... what do you use? Cards?'

'Aha. The Tarot. I've helped young women stop their marriages break up. I've helped young men away from suicide. I've done it only for good, not for gain. White magic, not any hocus-pocus, son.'

Stone kept his peace.

'I do a kind of theoretical, mental Tarot of everyone I meet. It's like a compulsion. You know I can see auras, I can see the bodily aura around everyone I meet? It's distinguished by colours. Grey is healthy for instance. Other colours portend Death.'

Stone shook.

'Oh?' he affected indifferently. 'And what would... what would say mine be then?'

'Eh? Oh grey, grey. Yours is healthy all right.'

'I don't believe it...'

'But you're not a settled man. Am I right?'

'My face would tell you that,' assented Stone dryly. 'I know that myself without the Qabbala.'

'You're eh... for ever going from one thing to the next, never settling. Wanting this, that, the other. Am I right?'

Stone agreed to the obvious, while scratching around for some means of qualifying the tortuous, hence forgivable, nature of his unebbing greeds.

'Wanting and craving is all to hell,' Dukes explained calmly. 'It's the wrong way to tick. You need to realise you have all

65

you'll ever have and to give up whatever you've got. Do you follow?'

Stone grunted cynically. 'I have needs,' he whispered, embarrassed to be talking so loudly in such a place. 'Addictions you might say.'

'Drugs?' asked Dukes commandingly.

'No,' scowled Stone. 'Women. Every one I see. I want *every* woman I see.'

'That's crazy,' opined Dukes.

'I know. Of course it is.'

'Restrain yourself!'

'I cannot. How can I?'

'Everything comes to the man who waits,' muttered the homely Confucius. 'You shouldna be so greedy.'

'It's all right for you,' grumbled Stone pettishly. 'People who don't hanker don't hanker. People who do, do.'

'Willpower,' asserted Dukes firmly. 'Find some way of giving up whatever you have. Christ man, a man like you as tender and soft as a babbie - when have you ever had all the easy *twat* you've wanted? Aren't you just all eyes?'

Stone flushed for shame.

'Find a good woman,' advised Dukes sharply. 'To hell with the rest. You know women like Kate? She's a player! She plays! You want love and she only wants to play with weakly men.'

'How do *you* know?' objected Stone indignantly, though his quivering voice belied his grumble.

'Folks never change,' Dukes explained assuredly. 'Let's say if by a miracle you was to marry yon Katie lass tomorrow, she would still be... yon Katie. She'd still be flighty, fooling, all for the good time. She would drive you stark mad within a week.'

Dukes led them back to the quay, Stone as good as tottering. The Qabbalist had been throughout his analysis gentle and pitying. Stone was shaken up from tip to toe. Here he was judged, weighed, measured, his motives laid bare, his fancies seen for the idiocies they were.

'But - what are your beginnings?' asked the Lowlander curiously, as they leant against the harbour rails. 'Where did you come from? You were no born with a spoon in your maw like Katie?'

Stone explained his origins, his roots. The village, the small house, the small parents, the small past. He related it as if it dealt with someone else. Such was his quaint relationship with himself in fact.

'Don't you keep in contact?' asked old Dukes, touched by the picture Stone painted from his amnesia.

He shook his head and said with conviction that he hated them. Dukes clicked his tongue with disapproval. He asked him why on earth was that. Stone admitted he had forgotten exactly why but there was good reason whatever it was. Disagreements, disaffection, treachery in the name of concern. What was 'kin' but enemy? Wasn't that true for everyone too, he asked Dukes sharply.

Dukes eyes greyed over again with pain. His own youth was rising up before him. And what desolation! Stone's own churning innards could not help but be moved by that suffering aglow in old Dukes.

'My ma was a whore,' Dukes grinned weakly. 'And my pa was a drunken fool. You see while you - by the sounds of it - was squashed and coddled in the name of love, I was left to live on fresh air.'

'Neglect,' said Stone.

'It's a word,' agreed Dukes. 'It's just a word. So is hell. Hell's just a word eh? You should taste the experience, son. You should taste what it's like for a wean to be neglected.'

Dukes steadied himself. He lit a cigarette and then advised Stone to seek reconciliation and to dissolve his hatreds. The occultist recommended the written letter as the best means. He said that a man who gave tit for tat was not a good man, two wrongs do not make a right and so on. All this made Stone melt more and more until he felt he was simply liquid. Meanwhile Dukes was leading him back by foot to the village where they both were camped. It was ten miles and they walked it all bar two. En route Dukes came out with his metaphysics and Stone listened far from credulously. Nevertheless he kept saying over and over to himself... *The Road To Emmaus*. Dukes talked of auras, how they were elastic and left the body during sleep and at death. How oak trees were rich in aura-substance and hence their vivifying shade. He believed that the Bible had been written by 'someone' only intent on giving allegory, a fable world, not the scientific truth of things. He conflated Mohammed, Buddha, Jesus, Lao Tse, and then went on to a theory of extraterrestrial government by fully aural spirits. Stone might have been melting throughout but his intelligence told him he was listening to drivel. This Dukes was a mixture of savvy and nonsense, of discrimination and absurdity, was how he interpreted. Stone might be having all his chocks pulled away, the corks pulled loose in the name of charity and generosity, but the wisdom of the mechanic involved was of a crankish, cosmic sort. It was too cosmic, too easily universal and all embracing by half.

Dukes invited the young man to his lair in the bracken where he anxiously prepared him a supper of beef stew. They had walked eight long miles and their legs were weary and their skins both tanned like ancient furniture. There was no more any hint of sexual overture from Dukes. The Lowlander whittered nervously as he peeled the vegetables and brewed some coffee. Here in his seclusion he was a little pathetic, more than a little broken. He was a lonely middle-aged bachelor. He was a solitary homosexual. His anxiety was lest his guest depart unannounced. Thus he coddled Stone and would not let him stir nor help him in any way. Stone was the laird and Dukes was his manservant. Yet over and above that the evening was of such fine clarity and beauty. They were by the enormous, frozen cerulean bay, its belly as great as the belly of God. It was so immense they melted into specks. They were cut off from all view, the road invisible, the traffic and by-passers dissolved. Here they had their nook and the smell of wood fire, the scent of salty stew in the odour of cooling bracken. There was a richness to life and to its possibilities that made young Stone melt even further. Everywhere he looked were miracles. And yet the miracle was he was literally dissolving like this day itself.

Early the next morning Stone departed without word to anyone. Without telling Dukes nor Kate nor any others he slipped off to the other side of the island, down to *Muile's* south west corner.

Whether it had been Dukes' confessions and donation of advice - if advice was what it had amounted to - that had precipitated a kind of internal dissolution, or whether such dissolution had been fated by the years that went before, or whether both or whether neither, Stone did what all of us do when cornered - he bolted like a rabbit.

He hitched two lifts and finally took a bus. Waiting for that bus he had observed a wrecked fishing boat rotting in an estuary of cracking mud. This made him anxious and uneasy, innocent a sight as it was. The old wreck had been as good as melting in the scorching midday sun, just like Stone himself. However, by early afternoon he had arrived at the village where the ferry departed for the isle of Iona, of *I*. And when Stone observed *I*, just a stone's throw across the sound, he could not believe his tear-filled eyes. Firstly that it was so small, secondly that it was so green, thirdly that its gentleness was so brilliantly meek in the burning sun. It looked like a skylark, like a little lark turned into an island. The green was turquoise green, the colour of Christ knows, but not an earthly green. Nor was it 'extraterrestrial' he thought to himself contemptuously. Stone breathed deep to have escaped the presence of crankish Dukes for he was so glad to be on his own again. He looked to *I* as if to a magic land. He saw its magic, its green goodness like a lark stretched out in the bay.

An astonishing interlude occurred just before Stone took the ferry across to *I*. As he turned from the piece of cheese and apple he was consuming, there about five yards before his eyes was the alarming presence of Kate the barmaid...

Stone could scarcely breathe at the sight. For she should be at least forty miles away by rights. From the vision of gentle, violently gentle *I* to this vision of violent, gently violent Kate. She smiled at him with a full sweet countenance. Today she wore a sleeveless shirt and her arms glowed blonde with the little hairs that shone upon their surface. Her presence breathed...

'What?' he murmured drunkenly.

Kate laughed gaily at his stupefaction. Stone laughed back with assurance, a queasy assurance. Melting in the liquid of remorse as he was, his contrition for times past, roots, history... himself, has he to discover it?.. he was confronted with the Qabbalist's demon, *the flighty woman,* card one thousand in the pack not quite invented. His belly lurched for possession. She had followed him, it was as simple as that. Her eyes twinkled with the same gentleness as the appearance of *I*. Stone knew she was profane, of course he did. Her mouth lines were calculating, her very gaze was devious. She confused good and bad wittingly, she was as bad as the worst of them. As indeed was Stone. As indeed was Dukes, who hankered plentifully himself. He hankered after hankering young men. Kate hankered after foolery and teasing, after spurious power. Stone held out his neck for lustful decapitation.

'It's my afternoon off,' she glinted. 'I have to return inside an hour.'

'How did you know I was...'

'The manager saw you. He was driving the other way, and saw you get onto the ferry bus. Why on earth did you make such a bolt for it?'

'Dukes,' said Stone honestly. 'I got sick of his presence. He was after me. He was. He was literally.'

Kate laughed riotously at that. Stone's dancing lust made him cannibalistic. He would have been content to eat her in carnivorous portions. Sure enough she had quixotically driven the forty miles behind him, tailing him for obscure ends. Just for the diversion. Now she was due to return the way she'd come. She had borrowed the dupe's car while he was walking in the mountains near Salen. Her companion Jane? Oh she was in the shop buying ice cream. Ahah. Meanwhile Stone's ferry for *I* was fast approaching, one that shuttled to and fro all day, until early evening when the bay here was deserted.

Had she tailed him in order to make one last bootless act of self-abasement manifest itself in Stone? He entered the ferry, no more than a full-size rowing boat, and waved goodbye to Kate. She waved goodbye perhaps affectionately. Startled, doltish looking Jane reappeared with ice creams from the store. She noted Stone and nodded nervously, half-guiltily towards him. She was no more than Kate's accessory, her unthinking inferior partner. Stone rued the fact that he had not stayed behind at the hotel to frustrate himself some more. Certainly if there had been no Dukes about he would have consented to stay there for ever. Such is the attraction of the never-arriving.

Here was peace that actually did pass understanding, on this isle off this island off the largest island. On its northern inhabited end where there was village, hotel and a field for campers, even in this most bustling part there was a vast serenity of tranquil meekness. Godless Stone mocked adjectives like sacred and blessed yet even he was obliged to search for a word that penetrated to this core of peacefulness, sheep, and sanded bays, whose plangent cream and dappling turquoise water were enough to make him doubt his own capacity to doubt. Whatever it was that he doubted.

There was an old and ruined abbey near to the jetty and further off lay the New Abbey, a place constructed in ancient style for present devotional use. The island was something of a pilgrimage place for religious individuals, who wandered about in cheerful groups, engaged in this or that residential course or earnest, loud discussion group. They, like Dukes, gave Stone the hab-jabs. He could see what they were after, God himself no doubt, but such a target seemed a long way away from fervid chatter and this boneless good humour. He had heard the rumour that God was great and terrible while these souls here were surely far too voluble and puny. They never stopped talking. They were always, always pleasant. Fortunately it was easy to get away from them. Away from the café and the Abbey were near-deserted beaches, lonely paths, small patches of gold sand hidden away by protruding rocks and stones. There one might have been spied by a telescope from *Muile*, but otherwise complete privacy was assured.

Soon evening came on, twilight stole across the field where Stone was camped. There must have been twenty tents, all at generous spacings from each other. There were no Christians here, thank God. There was an instrument being played but it was unobtrusive. The light became frozen and more concentrated, the acoustics stretched out miraculously across the bay between *I* and *Muile*. Seabirds pierced the evening like stars. On *I* there were corncrakes and they scratched their throats and the scrape of their crake thumped through the evening like a hammer. One blow after the other. It was like nothing on earth nor in heaven. The sheep chewed quietly and the suffocating tranquillity of the place became almost too much to bear.

Stone obeyed the Qabbalist. Outside his tent he took out some notepaper and wrote a letter to those he had offended and those who had offended him. Self-conscious a process as it seemed, he found forgiveness rather an easy task. It certainly did not feel like his usual 'nature'. All the while he wrote his letter, in fact all the time since that discussion yesterday afternoon with Dukes, he had felt himself becoming more and more liquid and contrite. But about what? And why? The corncrake scraped and gave the answer. Because, because, no more, no more...

He rose from his duty and took his letter down to the Post Office in the village, the small shack of a place where faded old black and white postcards - tinted turquoise where the sea had been photographed - were arrayed inside the window. He passed by the tumbled ruins where Columba had built the first abbey. Stone stopped and felt his own collapsing, ruined self. St Columba and his followers had sailed from Eire and landed at the bay down the bottom coast of *I*, a surpassingly sacred place Stone had been informed. Soon he would go down there and look seriously about him for all the evidence.

He continued up to the New Abbey. In its surrounds was a tumulus where the ancient Scots kings, including Robert The

Bruce, had had their bones interred. And Macbeth too? Around those grounds were numerous Celtic crosses, planted like miniature saplings, most of them only replicas of destroyed originals. The shape of the Celtic cross was remarkably endearing to Stone. He found that shape beautiful, heart-warming and proper to this isle, the essence of the very gentle, the spirit of *I*, and even of himself in some furthest reach of his dissolving self.

He entered the New Abbey, or rather walked into its inner quadrangle which turned out to be similar to the cloisters of an Oxford college. He skirted the church itself and walked the perimeter of the quadrangle, stopped to read at this or that notice advising the pilgrim devotees of a certain conference or a discussion group. Such information, all those *ciphers* of information seemed to Stone nonsensical. Why *confer* in such a place? Just to breathe the air was surely sufficient. Their severe chatter and earnest clusters and gossiping made him feel the ubiquity of language-obsessed humanity. Which filled up the spaces from Reykjavik to Mongolia with this incessant furious garble. As antidote to which what was kinder than Death, than dissolution into the speechless elements? Nothing whatever meditated Stone, for all the nostrum made him panic. Being so labile, so fully volatile as now he found himself, he was in no position to see these matters merely academically.

Small Celtic crosses were at the corners of the quadrangles, almost like planted shrubs in their postures. A single cross was fixed in a corner, raised up beside the stonework of the Abbey. It was made of some hard metal instead of the usual stone. It was long and thin and gleaming. It looked powerful as a dagger in its way. Behind it shone a candle, a clear, small, luminous, powerful flame. In strength is meekness and in meekness strength. Was that Dukes whispering into his ear from all of forty miles away?

He entered the church like some stealing mendicant. It was dark and virtually empty, the twilight had made artificial lights already necessary. It was a gaunt, gigantic building, tantamount

73

to a miniature cathedral, and the scent within was one of dust, wood, cooling stone, human bodies in a different state than if they had congregated for washing or shopping or debauchery. Two or three people were praying in the aisles. From a hidden recess there was a record playing loudly, a Peasant Mass sung in Spanish. It was evidently some South American villagers who were crying with heart and soul...

Señor, Señor, Señor!!!

That Peasant Mass was more than beautiful. It was quite overpowering. It filled up the church like flame itself. Stone felt no wish to pray but the power and intensity of that Mass was sufficient to take away all the strength in his legs, what minimal strength survived after these astonishing twenty-four hours. The weakness of earlier had become almost complete faintness of limb. He collapsed into an empty row of distant pews. He felt mutable, unhinged and quite strongly in personal danger, even if he knew neither from what nor whom. From hocus-pocus? Or from the Señor himself?

He felt his heart beating very violently. It was the *passion* in that music that made him feel in some obliquest way *he* was enduring an execution himself. The sweat was beginning to flood from his armpits and neck. If he had not known otherwise he would have felt himself in fever. But fever was something of the Orient, not of the Occident. In any case he knew the difference between fever and the other. This was the other. This was hocus-pocus, call it what you will, subjection to forces beyond intellectual or physiological control. It was intimately connected with that homily from Dukes, also associated with the leaving of Kate the horned, fanged goddess who burnt little men up like a blast furnace. Stone could see in his mind already the young English dupe ascending a short set of steps into the flaming incinerating vagina of Kate. Not that the dupe's sex would enter Kate's sex but that she might subtly retract him into her womb like a birth effected in reverse, a uterine suction so to speak.

Such a grotesque conceit made Stone sweat blood. He started to shake in fact. No one could see a thing in the church of course, he was alone and yards from the centre of the building. Curiously the church felt not so much a sanctuary - as a violent melting pot. As if to *shriek* (just like that Mass!) that God, Hocus Pocus, Señor, call it what you will, is great and terrible and not to be mocked...!

Señor, Señor, Señor!!!

The peasants sang as if their hearts were in their very spittle. Those ecstatic peasants were all Señor, infused and powered by the man, not by elastic aura, Dukes, muttered Stone rather madly. No, it was not the likes of Dukes was orchestrating this, not at all, but something that mastered Dukes was presently mastering Stone as well. Dukes was in all likelihood playing father to the young dupe right now and rescuing him from capricious Kate. Perhaps he might even succeed in bringing him to the arms of the tender, neglected wean that cried out for pitiable young men to caress and lend comfort. Good luck to them both thought Stone confusedly in his panic - but who will be *my* father today, Señor?

Señor, Señor, Señor!!!

He stared terrified at the stained glass that covered the far end of the Abbey. Bright green, rich blue, fiery yellow, burning white. There was such power in sheer colour, in bare physical elements such as those. His eyes tried to focus on the figures upon the glass. There was a Christ with woe and compassion upon his anguished face. His lips were flecked with blood. Yet Stone's eyes refused to adapt, or accommodate. He actually gaped as the colours there began to melt, to run free and trickle down and down like drops of... life?

Now he knew his own recent melting to be such a poor imitation of the Señor's; the destructive melting into compassion he had undergone since the discussion with Dukes. For this man has aptly been called Stone. To feel pity cost him the strength of his legs and arms. To take pity cost him the loss of his limbs. For who on earth was ready to become an invalid, in order to afford this crippling pity, the sheer effort involved in feeling compassion? Why, it was monstrous! It was...

At this point a troop of teenage mongols entered the church, open-mouthed mental-handicap patients being shepherded by some kindly and fatigued-looking superintendent. She had brought them here on pilgrimage these charges with their excess (or was it deficit?) of chromosome. They went to their pews and opened their mouths even wider. They prayed. And yet, thought Stone, not one of them could mouth the word chromosome! Wasn't that remarkable? How had their malady been explained to them then he thought hysterically? How on earth?

Their motleyness appalled him. The pity at that motleyness was crucifying. It was too much for gravid Stone. Gravid in the particular sense of ready for parturition.

Stone scuttered from the church, choking on pity. By now it was dark, the quadrangles filled with - look at them! - blazing Celtic crosses. It was black as hell save for the few torch-illumined crosses grinning at him in that deserted quadrangle. And Stone was filled with mortal terror, nothing less! He was on the run, the cry of that heart-tearing clutch of Latin American peasants, bawling to:

Señor, Señor, Señor!!!

Terror has a stage where it turns into apprehension of imminent death, of annulment. Stone's terror, as he stood with palpitating heart in the empty cloisters, rose to such heights of mounting limitless blackness that the horse of death appeared before his eyes and began to snort and pitch its hoofs against his dilating panic-stricken eyes.

Stone ran. Stone scuttered. He dashed from one end of the cloisters to the other - and then back again twice as speedily. Laughably, he disguised it as a nervous restlessness for any hypothetical audience, for he covered his tracks very smoothly as a rule. The Abbey was empty though, the island was fully deserted at that very moment. At these precise moments the world is swallowed up and all that is left is... terrified prayer...

'Oh Christ!' went Stone in bilious terror. It was a vocative embarrassedly disguised as an exclamation. For even in mortal terror, Stone maintained his 'human' pride.

He swooped on the metal cross of *I* that looked like a

dagger, and clutched at it, desperate for support. As the horse approached with steaming breath he clutched the harder and grasped as at a lifeline. He even begged for deliverance, though in an underbreath. After all, even if he was dying, there might be someone listening, there might be a danger of cynical eavesdroppers was his ludicrous anxiety.

The terror focused to a point where Stone *did* experience the tunnel of his death. The horse reared and bellowed in time with the Spanish Mass, the music suddenly stopped and the horse went up in a puff of smoke. Whereupon Stone died and felt his veins suffused with the energy of a white and sprightly mare. He knew in a word what faith meant. He went from the end point to the beginning, all in a twinkling and without an inch budged. In doing so he actually laughed out loud for with fire's clarity he saw that his death was indeed only of the imagination. It was nothing more! He had gone from mortal terror to immortal freedom in a second's grasp. And this thing mortality only existed as a thing imagined. Once attained it impishly turned itself inside out and dissolved into, among other things, riotous bellyaching laughter.

Stone left the Abbey on wings of mercury. He flew, or rather his feet took wing and bore him the quarter mile on to the deserted little beach, the *Traigh Bhaigh* for want of a name. For the man who had died was filled with what could only be called an excess of joy. It would have been an impertinence to call such a thing happiness. Or even bliss, which means nothing these days as far as one can gather. A great exultant joy took hold of his body, thin, dismal, stringy an appurtenance as it was, and put such vigour into his feet that Stone was tempted to actually hum and dance with joy.

In fact he did. Stone danced with irregular whoops on the plashing white sand in the pitch dark summer night, alone, free and unafraid, and beyond the call of all anxiety. Someone had left a little beach fire burning and upon it drunken Stone pissed with a fearless charity. For the first time in twenty years he had no jot of anxiety for *time* - such as in brooding for the past, anticipation of the future, cares for friends, delights of sense or

77

lack of such. He found it a great effort to fix his mind on his cares as he danced. He found it hard to fret as he leapt and whooped. He experienced difficulty in feeling short of anything throughout. It was a problem for him to blame or criticise person x or factor y. It was all a mystery. Yet this mystery had *no* portentousness. That was *real* mystery. It was all most richly humorous. Now he could even see who the great Señor was. Sometimes (only sometimes!) the Señor liked to dance, to laugh with vast hilarity, to turn everything inside out so that the dire was beautiful, the anxious trifling, the lugubrious comical, the phantom Death the phantom Life. The Señor was the end of hell and the start of paradise; the arse of a cat and the outrageous beauty of Kate. And words, words were such poltroonery, such feeble foolery. What beat the taste of this, what beat its very flesh and savour?

After his shaman's dance, Stone lay down and sank into great exhaustion. He felt such fatigue as only comes once in a lifetime. The concussed, the unborn and the blissful know this. He dragged himself feebly into a hidden-away cove, just far enough away from the fluctuations of island tide, and there collapsed into depthless torpor.

Before hitting sleep he saw ramming pistons, whirling gigs, fast moving trains, steaming rockets, flying trapezes and other violent images. He remembered the books of Ezekiel, Hosea and Daniel. On reflection he rued the fact he was not a Jew. He sank into the exhausted man's sleep and lay there thus for a good twelve hours.

The next day dawned upon a weary child. Stone was as weak as liquid, as if suddenly recuperant from fever. The memory of last night's adventure was returning and the erstwhile contemplative began to panic at such violent revelation. His neck thudded with alarm. He tried to disbelieve it, to write it off as dream. Then all of a sudden he disdained his unnecessary fear. For now he was sure enough himself again. Why, he found himself worrying about his tent, his breakfast, his plans for today and tomorrow and so forth. That was Stone, was it not? Whereas last night he had been crazily exalted and beyond such things of the world, such crass *laukika* concerns.

Here he lay in his hidden cove, an innocent sunbather. The morning's heat had made him even more nut brown and tanned. Here he lay on *I*, island off an island off an island, with his adventure in the past tense and all safely hidden away. No one knew anything of any of this, except perhaps Señor and except perhaps - though he doubted it - Dukes with his occult sensitivity.

Hence it was fiction and secret fiction at that, fiction unwritten and thus fable. No one would believe him back there on the *big* island, not unless they put that magic down to a nervous phenomenon or an excess of intoxicants. Despite the fact that Stone had had no more intoxicants than a few glasses of beer several days ago. Or some would refer to it as an adventitious phenomenon related to the nervous system. That the Señor was just a dose of nerves, an exercise in biophysics and neurology. Stone began to laugh. Or a hell of a lot of aura according to Dukes! Stone laughed even more. He guffawed like a madman. Sufficient of last night's power was with him still to scorn the profanity of this 'society' of his that ignored the like of Señor. Apparently it took wretched peasants in some blood-drenched capital like Bogota or Lima to put any passion and blood money by the Señor! Even occidental Tarotists were weighed down by an excess of polysyllabic junk. Stone sneered as he thought of Dukes reading his Tarot and lusting after frail young men. The religious and the profane so acutely paired and prostituted....

He raised himself onto his shoulders and stared about him. This rock surround had a fissure that allowed him to peer beyond onto the lovely white desert dune sand that was more like the Peloponnese than Scotland. The water's turquoise had a purity and pellucidity that took him back to infancy, to the stage where without effort he had known some of last night's freedom and hilarity. How at age four he would have been overjoyed at the sight of that water, the feel of that sand, the power of this sun. In fact it was not that last night's visitation had come mysteriously from outside, but that it had long years lain inside and had been part of the man that tasted it then for a few hours.

He stared too at the groups of people sucking up the sun. About twenty people were scattered in twos, threes and a couple of loners. His eyes took sweep until... the signal came. Then - the predictable occurred. One of the loners proved to be a young woman and automatically commanded Stone's hungry interest. As soon as he saw her he wished to be in her company. It was his disease, as shamefully admitted two days earlier to old Dukes the man-lover. See what a thin, scratty little woman she was. Twenty years old he guessed and with a nose that was too big for her face, a chin too thin and too forward-reaching. Her hair was short and she might half have been a boy. There was meekness in her eyes, a shyness which told Stone that she was either a foreigner or even local. She had such gentle homeliness upon her face. She had a slight vulnerable cast to her left eye which immediately endeared her to him. All alone she sat as he too sat all alone. He knew of her while she knew nought of him. That needed sharply to be rectified. For even with Dukes' admonitions in his ears he sensed with conviction that this was a good woman and were he to tell her that last night on this very beach he had tasted what lay beyond death, he would not have been casting his pearls before swine. This woman *was* a good woman, that he knew. How did he know? Why, by her eyes, by the spirit that shone in those unassuming, humble eyes.

Limp-limbed Stone arose, dusted himself down, went down to the green sea, the pure dream of a child's ocean, and proceeded to wash himself unseen. He finished by gargling and expectorating some sea water by way of cleansing his palate. He patted down his spiking hair and proceeded out from his cove, remembering too that Dukes had been a man for his seclusion. Nor was it too much of a spurious gambit to walk towards the young woman and inquire the time in a friendly voice. For he did want to know how long he had slept, how close it was to lunch-time and so on.

The young woman looked up expectantly and smiled. Her

eyes squinted in the dazzle, for Stone's head was framed by the sun. She commented humorously on that. Her thinness he found most amusing. Her gaze twinkled like a small beck inside the woods. He could see an animal, perhaps a deer or hare in there, inside her eyes. He recalled Indian poetry, the does, the doe-eyed, the gazelle-face, the fawn-glance. Down in his navel the songs were being born, the music making ready. This time he went beyond himself into tenderness. She had such a bonny yet motley face, this woman. Her voice spoke of *Glaschu*, nor was she well-spoken; she was a woman of the humblest background, he could tell by the way she responded. She had a thick accent. She said of all words *jings* as an exclamation at her own clumsiness in trying to find her watch inside her bag.

Stone who was as a rule a most hopeless gallant, sat himself down beside her in a friendly, companionable way. This was taken naturally and approvingly by the sunbather, who introduced herself as Mae. She was a music teacher she told him. She taught little ones up to the age of eight years. Stone confessed he would have forecast all of that. Mae bristled and laughed, in a generous way. Stone bristled and laughed also. It is not often one wishes love to out and sing after a few sentences like this, but Stone did right enough. The eyes and nose of Mae also seemed to want something. She was a woman of simple unaffectedness, an easy, modest type. Stone indeed could easily see her tantalising the pupils with her music, the presents they would bring her.

How was he supposed to understand this falling in love with a young stranger in the summer? This five days of roaming hypnotised and handlinked on an island that is baked by a mediterranean heat; a landscape no bigger than a village and surrounds, or an Asian tribal area, with the old and new abbeys as uncompromising landmarks. How they would sit in the busy café and just gaze at each other like animals. How they raced - as in hackneyed films - to the comical little *ceilidh* on *I* and danced folk dances to the sound of ancient reels on the record player. They danced like mythological lovers. When Mae danced she did it like a Hellenic gymnast, attuned, most graceful movements. She melted in his arms like a bird to its mother. She was a head shorter and nuzzled like a lamb to Stone. Stone softened with the contours of a throbbing heart. It affected everything. His body became a kaleidoscope of sorts. Mae turned out to be in the company of some women friends - though they gently left her to her adventurous romance. She would come to him, then return to her friends in the tent, then come to him again, then back again. He kept to his tent and kept it open for her. There was so much simplicity to this affair that it would have touched the devil. Yet Stone told her nothing of his encounter with the horse in the abbey. He told her very little. The elements were so strong in this island, light, heat, earth, water so aglow with their own unstarved powers that speech became a superfluity. They spent whole hours in easy silence. Their sex was as rich as bright apples. Yet they did not make love until the second or third day and when it was done it was more of a rite than a selfish passion. Stone's heart spurted tenderness, pity, affection in great waves. Mae melted beyond meltings. Her small face went beyond itself into child, infant, embryo, female homunculus. Stone watched her ontogeny and phylogeny as if she had been a butterfly turned from imago to the final fluttering miracle. Their love affair was not believable. It did not believe itself. It was magic, pure fiction...

They lay in the secluded little bay where Stone had slept off his earlier miracle. They lay breast to breast, her paps as sweet and small as little birds. Stone kissed her nipples and sucked the juices. They forced some fever into each other. No one saw. No one knew. There were only yards between them and the world and yet no one knew of the seeds and the eggs that met and turned into a zygote of... magic. Then when twilight came on they sat and stared at the Treshnish Isles, small fibrillating animalcules, small zygotes drilling dark blue as the sun sank down. Lunga, Fladda, *Bac Mor.* They walked out to them in their imaginations and lived alone as lovers left the earth. No trace then of Mae or Stone, simply evanesced into the skies or that into which the sun disappears.

Until Mae departed, as ordained. For she had her home to go

to, a future, the rest of her twenties. Stone too had to move on to what the Gaelic-speakers call *Tiriodh*. It was all planned long since. They parted thus with virtual haemmorhages, knowing it was all of the place and the time and the memory. It didn't have to be said. Each had a future and a world of his own making.

The day after she had gone back home with her companions, Stone departed for *Tiriodh*. But the final afternoon on *I* he took himself down to the delicate bay where Columba had landed - and sat stark alone at the end of the isle. He gazed across to the empty ocean. It melted away into whiteness, lostness and absence. The rock pools that bordered the bay were red, green, grey, jasper, agate, the stuff of speechless millennia. Bright hot sun fell on the little pools where the seaweed shone viridian and the crabs scuttered just as he had scuttered at the peasants bellowing to Señor. The heat turned the pinkness to goldpinks or the colour of the beyond, of the smile of Mae in embrace, the memory of all islands real and imaginary, a tinted picture of lonely Dukes staying safe in his guarded seclusion. Then it was that he stepped out onto the smallest rock which stood quite discrete from the bay. It was a rock off an island off an island off an island. Here at last Stone stood in true and fearless solitude.

Not At All!

Glee and his young wife were surely unwise to step so swiftly into the harp-builder's motorcar, particularly after that ferocious frown that greeted Mrs Glee as she dallied over tumbling into the front or the rear. The Swiss harp-maker scowled at her with humourless impatience, a strange expression from a silver-haired gentleman of sixty to a friendly-looking inoffensive woman of no more than twenty-seven. As for Mr Glee, the harp-constructor came racing around to the boot where he stood, curtly shuffled free some space for their admittedly bulging rucksacks... and shuffled with such ferocity and temper that Glee quite simply distrusted his senses. He thought he must be imagining that incredible irritability of the Swiss. Pardon him - inasmuch as it was eleven fifty-five at night and only a dim elemental light shone on the indistinct features of the Lugano instrument-maker. Also the fact that both Glee and his wife were fatigued and craving rest after a whole day's hitch-hiking from beautiful Firenze. Also that it made no sense that some elderly gentleman should offer a young couple a lift if he also intended to act like some Helvetian King Lear the whole way through the horrible journey.

It made no sense. Eventually Glee and the harp-maker were seated tightly in the front and weary Mrs Glee was doing her best to stay awake there in the rear. As spurious finale to his annoyance the old man slung forward the seat on which Glee was making unconfident motions of release. Glee wished to go forward because his wife's bag-covered knees were poking in the small of his back. The old man viciously jerked him forward with the scorn of a gymnastics teacher to procrastinating students. There was a horrible jolt. Glee's brains rattled in their anatomical casings. Meek Mr Glee laughed, his recipe for all ills (see the comical side of *everything)* appeasement being his ready watchword. Secretly he was amused, but only in the hysterical sense. It was black as carbide outside and inside he knew by some secret sense, he was seated next to a... God knows what? To be sure he could *smell* it, he could smell the odour of years-long...

'What is your destination?' barked the harp-maker disgustedly, after thirty seconds sniffs and silence.

'Eh?' stuttered Glee. 'Oh... to a campsite... the nearest campsite to Lugano that is.'

The old man had asked in German and Mr Glee had replied in English. This was partly because his German was so bad and partly because his wife knew none at all. He had also concluded his reply with a laugh, as if to imply he forgave the old gentleman's quaint brutality. The car meanwhile was spinning at eighty or so kilometres, the night was short on stars but big on dullness and impending rain. It was the beginning of September and they were cruising the motorway between Chiasso and Lugano. The mountains at last were asleep, unconscious in the cloaking dark. It was an area of his travels with which Glee had no sympathetic associations; Italian Switzerland, *Svizzera,* what precisely did that mean to him?

At Glee's laugh the harp-maker snorted. His snort was both nasal and of the larynx. It was the snort of torturers, maimers and theatrical devils. He succeeded that by a clipped cackle which genuinely made Glee's blood run cold.

'There are,' explained the old man tersely, still in fast and monotonal German, 'at least three or four campsites in the vicinity of the city of Lugano. Therefore - if you wish me to drop you off at one you must specify which one precisely it is that you signify.'

Must he? Mr Glee felt himself brightly blushing. Mrs Glee also flushed and tautened in sympathy with her husband. Not knowing one word of German only fostered her curious suspicions.

'Any one will do,' replied the young man mildly in his stumbling German.

'Excuse me - will you kindly repeat that statement!' demanded the harp-constructor amazedly, the quality of Glee's retort being too slight for his credible consumption.

'Any,' mouthed Glee uneasily, but again with a forgiving

chuckle. 'It doesn't matter which one. It really doesn't matter...'
A reeling pause...

'Wirklich's macht nichts!' thundered the driver, quite
apoplectic with his snort, so that his nose almost shot loose
from its bearings. *''S macht nichts!* Hah! To be sure! That's the
way! Why not? Hah! Isn't it the same with everyone! Eh! But
more especially the young folk, the *dear* young ones, who are
supposed to be tomorrow's leaders, politicians, doctors,
economists, philosophers, newspaper columnists and all the rest
of the bilge! It doesn't matter. *'S macht nichts!* Fah!'

He followed that interjection with a spraying expectoration.
He spat copiously at the dashboard. Glee was amazed. Mrs
Glee was greatly alarmed and begged of Glee *sotto voce* what
on earth the old man was spitting at.

'Don't worry, he's only cracked,' whispered Glee with yet
another bolstering laugh. He laughed for his own spirits, his
wife's spirits, even the harp-maker's peculiar spirits. He laughed
for all three of them, hoping to pacify them all thereby.

'You are English?' rapped the driver, wrenching the gear
stick as if it were a fairground slot-machine. 'Yes you are, of
course you are. What else could you be? But, do you profess
any other foreign languages? Or am I supposed to speak *yours*,
just as a matter of course, without debate, must I naturally fall
in with the parochialism of the English?'

Glee flushed once more, then nodded painfully, a negative,
'German,' he mumbled with the driest of lips. 'I speak some
German and I...'

'Fluently?'

Mr Glee paused and then limply muttered, 'A little...'

The harp-builder guffawed, almost screeched, as he threw up
his hands from the wheel...

'Ein bisschen! Excellent! Always, *ein bisschen!'* He stopped
and spat once more the limitless froth of his contumely. 'For the
Englishman it never differs! Every time one meets up with the
English, whether as hitch-hikers or in cars or in conversation on
the streets - or on the moon no doubt among astronauts - it is
always a *little* of this or a *little* of that. Why,' he snarled and
spat, 'can they not deign like everyone else to learn a foreign

language? Good God, it is such monumental, unforgivable arrogance! They come rollicking abroad and expect everyone, child and man, to speak English, and they in their asinine fatuous pride will go around muttering *ein bisschen, ein bisschen, un poco!* Everyone in the world must kowtow to the pride of the English, as if they are still the world masters controlling half the globe, no matter that they are now the world's *paupers* and come snivelling and begging with their...'

He spoke at such speed and with such slight regard for difficulty of idiom that it took all of Glee's reserves to concentrate and absorb the gist. By now Mrs Glee was in a frozen panic. Mr Glee's panic however took its invariable form of the hysterical laugh. He began to laugh and quake in nervous syncopation.

'Tell him to stop the car!' decided Mrs Glee firmly.

'It's all right,' mumbled Glee, craning his neck uneasily. 'He's only a lunatic. Really it's all right, he's only a crackpot...'

Mrs Glee groaned, leant back in her seat and richly sweated. Glee saw the bollards, the bridges, the faceless apparatus of the highway whizzing past on the almost deserted *Autostrada*. Of a sudden it took on its natural potential for bleak and empty nightmare. Then he blinked and saw himself and Mrs Glee with slitted throats, lying alongside the pitch-black roadside. It was such a vivid picture that he almost cried aloud. His benefactor meanwhile was expounding the lore of the polyglot.

'A man should be thoroughly fluent in at least one other foreign language, it is the most basic of *sine qua nons!* Otherwise he has not begun to be educated. I, in fact, am fluent in a good four languages, including English, which I refuse to converse in under present circumstances, but just to advise you not to lightly mutter towards the *Fräulein* - hah! - who sits there in the back. In case I should pick up a cynical inference is what I mean.'

At that hah! Mr Glee was stirred to hatred. That anyone, even a Swiss crackpot, should pour contempt on the head of his wife, a woman so patently gentle and reasonable that even a blind mute would have found some way of praising her generous temperament - that raised the cowardly indignation of Glee against the undeniable sovereignty a driver always wields over his hitch-hikers. He turned to the harp-maker and growled:

'She's my *wife*.'

'What!' started the driver.

'I said she is my *wife*, she is not *a Fräulein*, she is my wife and...'

'I do not doubt it, very well, it does not put me out of countenance that she is your wife! It is just that I give lifts very often to all classes of hitch-hiker, young, old, satisfied, querulous, ones who disturb me and ones who bore me stiff. Nine tenths of them - the couples I mean - are twosomes who doubtless have intimate relations, but who have elected to do without the formal ratification of the wedding ceremony. It makes a change indeed! It is a novelty! Monogamy!... And yet,' he gabbled, as he ruthlessly accelerated, 'tell me please, how long have you two youngsters been safely married? A month? Two months? A week...?' he noisily snickered, braking like a locomotive into horrible short snorts of amusement.

'Three and a half years,' counter-snorted Glee, sweating without cessation.

'And you are happy - I know for a fact! - with your little wife?'

Glee replied stoutly and shortly and limply that indeed he was. The harp-manufacturer then whittered inaudibly and praised Mr Glee with half-witted irony, just comprehensibly asserting that everyone he met was full of romancing lies and pointless deceit, it was the way of the fantastic, utterly ridiculous world. Still - what did it matter, to be sure *it did not matter.* The old man briskly tackled the phenomenon from all angles and in particular the aimlessness of the entire world, its lack of measure, content, rhythm, sensitivity, spirit. He muttered in a difficult German of lengthy abstract nouns, noted happily at one point that Glee was having great trouble in comprehension, and sneered: 'I can see your German is far from accomplished, Mr Englishman. But still - what does it matter? What *does* it matter?'

Mr Glee stiffened. His temper once more sparked and flared. As well as the fear common to all hitch-hikers that this time at last he had found the illustrious mass-murderer, first-class rapist, fine all-round hatchet man, dashing exposer, masturbator to outstretch all others etc., there was the reflex anger at finding oneself in this absurd situation of being abused and being humiliated. A hitch-hiker in fact had no power, and never would have. A hitch-hiker was required to take whatever was levelled at him by the donor of the singular relationship. There and then, for the thousandth time, Glee swore that he would never again hitch-hike, never, not even to save his life...

'Why the deuce did you give us a lift?' he addressed the harp-builder angrily. 'Why on earth did you pick us up? From the minute we got in this car you have been bitter and accusing. Why not leave us where we were, *um Gottes Willen!* Why on earth are you so incredibly angry?'

To Glee's surprise the harp-man trembled and faltered a little at such sincerity. Then he had the deviousness to deny his anger, then, after a pause, to affirm it, and finally to repeat again the insanity of anyone getting into a car for a lift without having *eine genaue Richtung* for the lift-giver. Mr Glee irritably, tremblingly repeated that the old man was inordinately enraged with them, he did not seemingly *like* his hapless guests. At which the old man snorted, presumably at the crude transitive relationship of 'liker' and 'liked' - that Glee should dare to imply a grammatical relationship between the driver and himself! - and then, without apology, bitterly began to recall the reason for this mood of his.

'Last night I was staying on business down in Milan,' he muttered at the windscreen, 'in a poky hotel where the noise from below my room was enough to fill a thousand-capacity concert hall. The transistor radio blaring with horrible popular music of such vulgarity it was even disgusted with itself, it could not face itself so to speak! It went on until three in the morning and all night long I had not a wink of sleep and perhaps, in some measure, that explains my irritable state of the moment. They were manual workers, bricklayers I believe, who were sleeping four in the room with drink, women, noise, their cooings and little laughs the whole horrible night through. Uproar of the nature of a convivial *party* - what is a *party* define that for me eh? - with laughs, shrieks, squeals and the Lord only knows exactly what manoeuvres in exactly what furtive corners...'

Mr Glee and Mrs Glee heard the smacking of the harp-maker's lips. They shuddered to their frozen cores.

'Are you married?' coughed Mr Glee feebly, having racked his brains for pacifying gambits. It was unthinkable of course, that such a slavering monster should ever have got near any woman...

'No!' replied the Swiss with a falsetto rectitude which eschewed all embarrassment. 'I am in fact a bachelor and most willingly so! I live up high in the mountains near Lugano with my three sisters, ageing spinsters all of them, and to tell the truth a surfeit of womanly company is my bane. Hah! Enough though of disclosures of that kind, thank you very much! Your case, your case is so different! It must be so favourable for you to enjoy the comforts of marriage and for three and a half years of unalloyed happiness with your charming young wife! You are, by the way, what age?'

'Thirty-one,' coughed the tourist.

'Your wife?'

'My wife is twenty-seven.'

'Such proximity! A young, helpful, caring wife! No, I live with the peckings of my three quarrelsome sisters, a bachelor who still maintains a vivid interest...'

'I'm sorry, but in what?' faltered Glee.

'They are old and full of arguments. They have no professions, nor meaningful passions. They bicker like speckled chickens over corn.'

It took the Englishman some laborious seconds to construe that particular simile.

'So how old are *you?*' he suddenly thought to throw at the driver in a defiant, impertinent voice.

The harp-maker ignored that very pointless question.

'Often, on several occasions, I have taken hitch-hikers back to my house up high in the mountains...'

Mr Glee translated in a whisper that last disclosure. The Glees blinked and palpitated as they stared at the dark and invisible heights.

'It is large and comfortably appointed. Old valuable furniture, large, warm, soft and comfortable deep beds! If I enter early for breakfast in the morning, I ask no police-style questions about who has slept where and I forbid my sisters to grumble at the table too. They get up to all sorts in the beds reserved for guests but I do not enter into it *nor* them. I make no bones about it! Although I say it *does* matter, my sisters say it matters much more emphatically than I. After all, they are not men of the world! *None* of them! I know through having travelled on business exactly what... practices...'

Mr Glee hurriedly interrupted to ask his profession and it was only at this point that he discovered the old Swiss built classical harps. The Anglophobe was a *Harfebauer...*

'For all the soloists and orchestras of note,' he grinned savagely. 'Every first-class harpist writes to me direct.'

'That is very specialised,' whispered Glee in sincere amazement, momentarily oblivious of the full horror of their situation.

'Indeed,' replied the old Swiss, ever so lightly mollified.

'And interesting,' flattered Glee with all his syrupiest unction.

'To be sure,' agreed the craftsman. 'A profession which one enjoys is a rarity and correspondingly to be treasured. I have built my harps for thirty-five years and put all my heart into every harp. I take my time and work always to perfection. If I don't achieve perfection then I achieve nothing. A half-good harp is like a half-good heart, it is a mockery!'

There was deep emotion in his voice. Mr Glee was almost hypnotised.

'It takes commitment,' the Swiss concluded - and then...

'Your own profession?'

Glee stated it.

'And your wife?'

Mr Glee explained with linguistic difficulty that she worked with people who had problems. People in the form of families, groups, individuals and so forth. Ten pregnant seconds of silence followed. And how could poor Glee have predicted the remarkable venom that such an innocent statement would ultimately have stirred?

'What!' roared the old man, spraying fresh volumes of his disbelief and rancour. 'Do you mean to say she works for the Red Cross with ministrations of soup and meat? Or is it something much more impressive and subtle? For surely *everyone* in this world has problems of one sort or another, and it is the current anomaly that now there are specialised agencies for helping only certain of these problematic persons. If you say she works with people having problems then I assume she works with the whole world, a busy professional what! One might say it is a Messianic role similar to that organised by such professionals - hah! - as psychiatrists, doctors, solicitors and so forth!

'In point of fact, no one has ever convinced me of the need for nor the authenticity of the profession of, *zum Beispiel,* psychiatry, the so-called psychological illnesses, to which I would respond that everyone has emotions and affections and that is their own business, there is no baseline nor means of tagging a person with this or that deficit or excess! There is simply human nature in all its throes. We all have problems and why not? Do you have no problems, Mr Polyglot? Isn't life a struggle between problems and their solution? Is that not *life* itself?'

He ended his declaration with a vibrant bellow. Glee had nodded, dazed, but in any case the driver was awaiting no reply. And by this stage Mrs Glee had had enough of remaining passive spectator of unintelligible Teutonic rage. The old man was again cackling away to himself and gibbering *'S macht nichts!* over and over again. Mrs Glee did not understand a word of it. Yet panic had raised her slowly to a defiant aggressor. She reached over briskly and shouted in his ear:

'Whatever it is you're muttering, just shut your damn silly mouth! You bloody old, ridiculous old fool! What right have you to pick us up and abuse us like this? You wicked old, bloody old, ridiculous old man!'

It was her biennial explosion. Even the gentlest souls know honest anger, a startling fact. Mr Glee silently applauded what he himself had not the courage to do.

'*Sozialarbeiterin!* A social worker!' gasped the driver, nodding his head with addled, twitching cynicism. Once more he spat at the windscreen. At this point Mrs Glee quivered and lanced him with an obscene word. She called him a...

'He called you a social worker,' interpreted Glee. 'He thinks it's funny you being a social worker and shouting at him like that. He imagines social workers are not supposed to...'

'Stop the car!' bawled the panic-stricken social worker. 'Will you... does he understand any English do you know?'

'He claimed he knew four languages in all.'

'Stop the car! Here! Or I'll scream my head off, you old bastard!'

The harp-maker guffawed more and more. He slapped his leg and again irrigated the dashboard in front of him.

'I suppose,' he twittered to Glee, 'that as a social worker she is empowered to have the people she does not like arrested. For instance those whose *Geisteskrankheit* - so called - hah! - she finds offensive. That being anyone who takes exception to her disarming vagueness which is prepared to take a free lift but not to give an honest destination! Good God! What if I said I *didn't know* where I was going in this car, I was just going anywhere and perhaps somewhere not to your arrogant English inclinations! Your monoglot pride! Your monoglot plus *ein bisschen* and I can tell by the strain in your posture that you are exerting every muscle to understand my speech. *Ein bisschen!* Well let me make it plain, my English hobos, *meine jungen Landstreicher!...*' he finished on a rising, terrible note...

The car then ground to an immediate halt. Both Glees shot forward in their seats. The harp-man sneezed and cackled. The Glees sat still in frozen terror. Here was the blooded end, wait

93

now for a knife, a gun, a crossbow, a scarf! Just outside... just outside, what was clearly... was that not a *campsite?*

Lugano was twinkling away in the distance, they saw the roadsigns to prove it! What? It took some seconds for Glee to realise as much - for firm there in his imagination he was expecting the appearance of a hatchet or a pistol or a mace. Mrs Glee was the first to recognise it as a genuine campsite and she leapt, panting from the car, with a snorting, trembling alacrity. Glee followed in a trance, still waiting for the blow on the back of the head from a harp or a ministering angel. Then to his amazement the harp-maker dashed around to the boot and emptied out their bags. More, he tutted old Glee out of the way with a most touching, old man's politeness. Such natural, genteel gallantry! He took out the ten-ton rucksacks and deposited them with a bow at the young couple's feet. Then grabbed Mr Glee's hands, pumped them warmly, and wished him all luck with his career, all success with his clearly happy and prospectful marriage! A *bon voyage* to England followed that. Then to Mrs Glee he extended a cordial uncleish paw and minced her sweating, defenceless palms with more sweetness than a thousand angels.

'*Gnädige Frau!*' was how he finally addressed her, and translated for her benefit:

'Most gracious lady!'

His accent was strong. Finally he repeated his invitation to the beautiful house on the hill, the swimming pool, the tasty snacks, the large, deep and comfortable beds. Then there were his records, or he might even perform himself, for he played the organ, he had a friend who was an *Orgelbauer* who had built him one in the music room, where he often sat and gave recitals to his three carping sisters...

He was too kind. Glee stuttered and thanked him with his legs a-tremble, his wife yanking him away into the safety of the campsite. The old man bowed once more and made a most meek and deferential departure.

''*S macht nichts,*' he whispered with the sincere charm of a friendly mountain dweller, then climbed into his Peugeot and drove away at speed to the dark and sleeping heights.

A Ticket to Bombay

She had a botanical name, Iris, a name which had other echoes of diminution, slowness and placidity. But this Iris, decidedly, was larger than life. And florally speaking she was more like some nervous forget-me-not... but rooted by the top of some blazing volcano. For Iris was full of dynamite, and wished to pretend otherwise. To pretend for example that she could live the life of a teacher when really she was destined to be a wanderer, an agitator, a curse on tired provincial conformity.

Iris suffered. She was in the advanced league of sufferers, had had two or three spells in the hospital, was now on monthly injections of Melleril, and to the world's satisfaction at least 'holding down' now a respectable job. Her job was as a teacher, of the little ones, a task which plainly wasn't her predilection but more a means of disciplining herself and satisfying such scrutineers as her father, her relations, her doctor, psychiatrist, and the eyes of the watchful community.

Everything about her was different and original. I met her because I replied to the advertisement she had placed in the Workington paper; that barefaced request for a tutor in Marathi. In Marathi! As if anyone in West Cumbria, where the sum total of immigrants must comprise perhaps three hospital doctors, most likely not one of whom would be from Bombay or near there, would hearken to her plea. Not that I knew Marathi either, I hasten to add. But at this period I was very poor and needed any income I could muster. I wrote to that box number at once and disclosed that I held a linguistics degree from an old university and that we might perhaps teach ourselves Marathi together. I added without unction that I doubted the correspondent would get any Marathi speakers in this part of the world. Even more to the point I was only asking one pound fifty per hour.

It was a good three weeks before there was any reply. She phoned me at the lonely cottage where I was temporarily dwelling and agreed to give our lessons a try. She admitted in a dull, confused sort of voice that she had had no other offers. My bright questions and comments seemed not to lighten the unease that was there at the other end. She spoke timidly, flatly, halting and without any learner's eagerness. The reason for her acquiring Marathi was that she had a boyfriend in Bombay who was a film-maker, and whose language she intended to know fluently. Yes, she already had acquired the *Teach Yourself Marathi* text, and would fetch it along when she came.

I was on my own at the time, and was pleased to hear a woman's voice over the phone. My anticipation ran away with itself as I saw a progression from text-book to pub to the sheets. That was - until I met her, and all thoughts like that went out the door along with the phutt of her dying motor car. It was a Cortina and on its very last legs. Iris here was anxious, apologetic, taut-wired, and evidently in need of gentle handling.

She was about five-feet-six, red-haired, pouchy-faced and pouchy-eyed in a pharmacological rather than congenital manner. There is a particular type of slitted cast to the eye, a special kind of plumpness in the cheeks and jaws, that is characteristic of certain medication, and which I recognised in her almost at once. It was only a week later she told me of the injections and related matters. Aside from that her eyes tended to stare, almost bulge from moment to moment, as if she had little control over whatever pressure was pushing behind them.

Those eyes in fact were jammed with fear, likely terror, and Iris always held herself as if she was about to slip, slide, sink and disappear from view. It was partly something as trivial and therefore as repellent as her being always on guard not to give offence nor be impolite nor make a mess. One imagined a stern training as a child or maybe a drastic and guilt inducing error at some recent point in her biography. As we worked away at our text, she showed herself as struggling, unconfident and easily crushed. Like a frightened child she needed so much patience, so much coaxing, and so much time.

I was not the best of teachers. I was gentle and uncritical mostly but also frequently brisk and bustling as I taught. After the first few weeks of novelty we came to that dead point where she would obviously get no further without a certain amount of spadework in the way of memorising vocabulary, grammatical paradigms and so on. Which she would not. It was something she attempted to brush aside as outside the possibilities of her schedule.

'I just haven't enough time, it seems to me,' she said, with a little dryness. 'I only really have the weekends and on Sundays I'm at my father's doing one chore or the other. On Saturdays I *need* to have some time off. I do my best to make time, but somehow...'

'It would take you ten minutes at most,' I said obstinately, and a little chiding at her evasions. 'We're getting stuck on the same two chapters because you don't know the basic grammar there, nor much of the vocabulary either. I mean...'

At which she fought against the looseness of her jaw and her eyes began to stare and her face started to flush and I felt for once quite brutal and insensitive. She mumbled something about having another determined attempt and we went back gingerly, eventually to the repetition of sentences such as, This Is A Light, I Live In A House In Bombay, The Servant Fetches A Meal From The Kitchen... and so on.

Iris was in her early thirties while I was just turned twenty-five. She had been a teacher for almost eight years now, she explained. For it was after the third lesson that she invited me into the nearest pub for a drink and insisted on paying for that one and the next. I had already hinted how poor I was in refusing this outing at first, and then again I did not wish to give her ideas. On the other hand I had had almost enough of isolation and solitary poverty. In the pub I reflected that I was surely as much an enigma to her as she was to me. Slowly she was getting less afraid and less self-watchful in my presence. It intrigued her that I was somebody making a determined effort to live by his art, when she could only make ends meet by doing her untantalising job. For Iris was also an artist as well as pedant. Ten years ago she had graduated from the Royal Academy after specialising in Fine Art, and now in between teaching and its preparation and all the other niggles and obligations that swallowed her time, she did sketches, prints, a little modelling and sculpting, all of which she marketed in a very humble way in the one or two galleries and gift shops that catered for Lakeland tourists with money to burn.

She would have liked in her dreams to be a full-time artist and let the teaching look after itself. It was an enchanting idea but it held its terrors. She thought that she might break down once again if she threw up the discipline of her job. The three breakdowns she'd had, had happened nine, six and three years ago, from which periodicity she expected to have another one soon. The association of merciless statistics and her fear of going mad by pleasing herself... all added up to a dreary, comfortless binding. The last two years she had travelled in India and Sri Lanka in the long vacations, and now she entertained unlikely sounding hopes of moving out there to live with her boyfriend, the film-maker, Prakash, where she would paint, sculpt, ride horses... and maybe not go mad again.

While at the Academy she had got involved with another art student, Randolph Street, a dark, moody, talented and impetuous man. It had been an attachment on her part which had felt the agonies of total rejection when finally he had plucked up the nerve to confess feeling dead to her for the last six months of their eighteen-month affair. It was a week after she had sat her final exams that he had finally got to mentioning it. There were a few horrible complications involving another woman being pregnant and her own flat being set on fire by a maniac jazz musician from the floor below. At any rate - she had cracked, right richly, with hallucinations, singing, nudity and more. And then, like a scourge, her anxious father had descended post-haste from distant Workington.

'I told him sitting up in bed I was going to get myself a flat in London and set out as a free-lance artist. But he wouldn't have that - would he hell! He instructed me I was going to get a Teaching Diploma and I was going to settle myself down. In his opinion it was the easy-going Bohemian life had led me to this breakdown, and that I was in need of some sort of secure background to regain the stability that was lacking...'

I laughed at her bitter sarcasm. It seemed she managed to loathe her father as well as pamper him.

'What does he do, your father?' I asked.

'Oh, he's a tax specialist. Half the Cumbrian businessfolk get him to cook their books.'

And his insistence coupled with her pathetically weak confidence had pushed her into that wretched teacher training. Her father had even insisted that the two year course must take place within a reasonable radius of Workington. He had offered her a choice of Newcastle, Manchester or Leeds for further studies.

'I lived in a solitary bedsit in Leeds for all that time. It was diabolical. It was so utterly bloody dreary.'

'Why?' I asked. 'Why did you give in to him?'

'Why?' she echoed, with pouting vehemence. 'Because he said if I started going off the rails and cracking up again, he would seek to have me committed *again,* for my own good.'

'Does he hate you?' I asked.

'No. Christ knows. He's querky.'

'Querky? That's most charitable. What about your mother?'

'She and he are separated.'

Iris then disclosed that she was the eldest of five daughters. On Sundays she drove over from her own little terrace in Mula, to that residence of his just outside Workington. There her father dwelt alone though with the occasional visits from a certain elderly lady-friend. Iris made him his Sunday dinner and stayed usually until late evening, and she also lent a small amount of voluntary assistance with his copious paperwork. Her mother, for whom she expressed little taste, she saw about a third as frequently. She was fond enough of all her younger sisters despite she saw little of them these days. They were all married, child-tending housewives, with husbands notable successes in the Midlands and Home Counties. She by contrast was in her thirties; fragile, frustrated, and without even a steady boyfriend. There was this connection in Bombay true enough, but it would be a minimum of another nine months hard saving, before she might fly out to stay with Prakash.

Just before the commencement of our tenth Marathi lesson - she was doing two per week at the special double rate of £2.50 - she presented me with a sellophane-covered dish of chicken korma she had prepared the previous evening. She blushed and smiled and rocked to and fro on her axis, as do certain Oxford dons. I thanked her shyly and a little warily. Two days later she arrived mid-afternoon with an invitation to come to supper that very evening. She was in a fluster of excitement as well as having scared and strained-looking eyes and cheeklines. She said that she would drive me back home afterwards as I sought for a hasty refusal. Then I remembered that someone was coming to visit me this evening whom I wasn't particularly keen on, so that an evening and a meal out with Iris would perhaps be a blessing in disguise.

Mula is as peculiar as its name suggests. Historically it had been the most sunken of all communities, that place where you were despatched if you could not afford the humble rents of those mining villages nearer Workington and Cockermouth. There were two or three similar colliery hamlets that had been the butt of jokes about dumping grounds and haunts of potters yet, even amongst these, old Mula had been the lowliest. This is to talk of the 'twenties, 'thirties, early 'forties when the rents at Broughton might be say eight shillings a week but at Mula only five and sixpence. Now, even in the middle of the 'seventies, it was still a name to elicit scorn and merriment.

It was in fact just a single and very long row of colliers' cottages, mid way down its length being met from either side by perhaps another half dozen dwellings. Its pub, as if half embarrassed, lay a good mile out of the village, stark in the middle of nowhere. Mula itself was just as topographically barren, lying like an anaesthetised caterpillar in desolate, windy commonland and at moderate elevation compared with the just visible and massive fells of the Lake District. Two miles away, down from the main road between Workington and Cockermouth, it could be barely spied as that long, straggling, broken locomotive of a place, pitch black and filthy from the pits; alone, pathetic, unappetising, more than a little frightening.

It was just the place for Iris to have settled it seemed to me then, though I was unaware at that stage that the housing scarcity was even turning dreary Mula into something approaching desirable. Before long it would have its quota of bungalows and modernised gew-gaws and Iris would only be one of the gathering caucus of teachers, social workers, and that same homogeneous, homogenising crowd of incomers...

She whisked me here just as dusk was falling on my cottage and as darkness was going to cover all of ugly Mula. The Mula streetlighting was so bad and the absence of stars and moon so utter, that I could barely see a yard before me. Everywhere was black, opaque, unyielding. There was just sufficient fog to help discern a freezing sodden vapour below the glass of the ancient street lamps. I managed to make out Iris' face as she turned to mutter some guidance, and just then that slanting strain in the eyes seemed all of a piece with the lugubrious atmosphere. Her house lay on a downward slope going crossways through the village, a little collier's cottage that had been purchased for a thousand pounds a few years earlier.

Inside she had decorated and furnished it in a tasteful, sensitive way, with pastel-painted walls and attractive pieces of inlaid, antique furniture. Samples of her sketches and prints were hung or pressed against the walls throughout. They ranged from stark lino cuts of mountainous landscapes - harsh and piercing in black and white - to watercolours of liquid-eyed elves or goblins with that same sorrowful, grief-frozen stare. She showed me a folder of cartoons and drawings. The jokes of her cartoons were quite beyond me. It wasn't that they were naive or unfunny as much as being pointlessly idiosyncratic and eccentric. Then there were her photographs of India and Sri Lanka. They were truly remarkable, most professional black and white studies of cave temples, street scenes, a funeral-burning, some ragged children, a one-eyed fisherman, and a smiling Indian film crew. Prakash turned out to be a handsome, boyish-looking thirty-year-old. He had his arm slung round Iris in jaunty, unIndian affection for the pose. She was smiling with a touching, full-faced delight.

She showed me her treasures and accomplishments with a nervous, hasty commentary and all the while stopping and looking uneasily for satisfaction or at least absence of disapproval. It was tempting to just take her hand and tell her there was nothing to be so afraid of, had it not been likely interpreted as a sign of a gelling affection. I was not so slow as to be unaware that she was getting very warm. While allowing sympathy and enthusiasm for what she showed me, I was most guarded in other ways. I could not completely relax a vigilance as I recalled the starless, foggy, desolate space that hung around these walls.

She had prepared an Indian meal of sautéed aubergines and cauliflower curry together with chapatees, pickles, yogurt and pappadums. It was very delicious and I gobbled it down with second helpings. She was pleased and her pleasure always took the form of a red face, full-throated laughter, and a mild hysteria. It was the nearest in fact she allowed herself to going mad outside of a hospital. She had provided plenty of drink in the way of cans of beer and a couple of bottles of sherry, and before long she herself was well benumbed. I sipped at my single large can of lager and met her spasmodic, unnerving giggles with a certain degree of phlegm. The second time this happened she chose to chide me.

'You're very serious. You are very serious, you know.'

I smiled and said nothing. She had spoken with a slight diagnostic and disapproving tone that would have irked me in anyone else less fragile. When it happened again she swallowed her merriment and then went glary-eyed and alarmed once more. In response I grew a little warmer, a little more sympathetic. She relaxed ever so minutely and turned to talking about books and poetry. She mentioned Blake and how much she revered him. She was a little surprised that I was not so acquainted with nor thrilled by his writings. I admitted blushingly it was more likely my deficiency than Blake's. She was also, she added, a devotee of both Milton and Donne.

'Do you believe in the spirit world?' she asked me suddenly, her eyes helplessly bulging again.

I paused to consider. 'I've got an open mind. I haven't myself met any spirits, mind you.'

'I have,' she said, straight-faced, though self-conscious at the pressure upon her eyes, trying a little to control that powerful stare.

'Have you?' I said a little uneasily, remembering the fog, the dark, the cold, the empty plain where Mula lay.

'You might laugh,' she said defensively. 'But I have seen a spirit that I recognised from a photograph. It's come to me twice - and I'm sure that it will again.'

Her eyes dilated - as did my abdominal veins and adrenals.

'Here?' I whispered, trying to appear sanguine, but almost bulging-eyed myself.

'No,' she said. 'Not here. It was at Workington. At my father's house.'

'Oh,' I said, exhaling, smiling at her almost affectionately.

'It was Prakash's mother. At the foot of my bed she stood. She *died* a year before I ever met Prakash.'

'Oh ,' I repeated, feeling a chill up my back as I had this image of an elderly saried dowager of Bombay standing at my hostess's bedside. 'Did she... what did she say?'

'Nothing,' Iris answered dreamily. 'Nothing. She just smiled. She stood by my bed, woke me there in the middle of the night, and stayed there radiating a kind of calm. She didn't say a word. She was only there for a few seconds I suppose. I wasn't afraid. Not even a little. It was as if she was a guiding spirit.'

I couldn't think what to say next. I even wanted to go into hysterics as I thought of Prakash's mother taking a trip from cosmopolitan Bombay to humblest remotest Workington. Even as the behaviour of a ghost it seemed a little impulsive.

'I once had fever and dysentery,' I told her after a pause, 'and one morning, just for a split second, I saw the most amazing sight. I woke up to see the head, the torsoless head, of this blond-haired albino child on top of my hotel room table. Its eyes were frozen and sweeping from side to side in a slowed down arc...'

103

She looked startled. 'Where was that? Was that in India?'

'In Turkey. In fact I'd seen exactly the same object in a Fellini film in Nottingham about two years earlier.'

Iris snorted.

'I wasn't in a fever,' she said coldly. 'I wasn't even on tablets at the time.'

In this manner she alternated all evening between coldness and hectic efforts to entertain and provoke. Thus she would dance between determination and frowning, and that pathetic and unfortunate pop-eyed glare. After a final discussion of Oriental religion, of which she had a sympathetic and devotional knowledge, professing to be a Buddhist if anything, I asked her politely if I could be driven home. It was a quarter to twelve and I was weary. Mula, its isolation, Iris' moods and fancies, were all making me very uneasy. I wanted to go home to solitude and safety.

She would not let me go. She insisted that I stay. I had to plead. She said with determination and a sorry stare that she would prefer to drive me back in the morning when the fog might have lifted. I would be doing her a favour she added. Her hands were clutched as if entreatingly. I felt blackmailed and just as determined.

'All right,' I said sharply. 'Which is *my* bedroom.'

The anxiety and despondency took over as she flusteredly gave me instructions of which way to turn at the top of the stairs, which plug to switch for the room heater and the electric blanket, which direction for her bathroom and so on. I turned at the bottom of her staircase to say goodnight, and saw that she was still half-hoping I might come out with it, or at least show a shy, unspoken willing.

'I'll see you in the morning, Iris,' I said as kindly as I could, and firmly.

'Yes,' she replied, stunned. 'Yes. I'll see you then.'

I lay half-awake all night, dreaming and turning fitfully. I was on guard for either Iris in the guise of a wild-eyed witch or Shree Prakash's venerable mother's ghost, creeping here into my bedroom. Iris I had heard stomp rather than walk up to her own room. She was hurt, annoyed and upset at my seriousness, my coldness, my indifference to a cost-free night of lust. I was also thoroughly riled at being kept here and forcibly pushed into something so hurried and brazen. I was just as testy as herself in the morning at the breakfast table. Her copy of *The Guardian* disclosed what I thought was a particularly savage jail sentence for a young Sinn Feiner and she flared for once as I expressed my furious disgust.

'He killed twenty people,' she said, 'barbarically. Innocent people.'

'He's twenty years old,' I replied. 'And all those years, three life sentences, are just as barbaric. A damn sight more. What use is savage revenge? And that's assuming he's guilty...'

The argument raged as she drove me back across the windy plain to my cottage. The world looked as bleak as the plain while we argued. It became apparent that her politics were a humbug mixture of entrepreneur and romantic, for she cited approvingly her ludicrous father's opinions as well as her own. Then she dropped me off politely but sourly. She was cold. I was cold. It would be another six days until our next Marathi class.

Her Marathi proficiency stayed at a constant low but she did not seem to mind. I was glad financially but bored with the lack of progress. As diversion and as teaching aid I'd acquired a set of records with Marathi conversation on them. Single words and then short phrases for pronunciation were repeated by what sounded to be a duo of endrugged septuagenarians. One of the elders had a soprano, the other a bass and husky voice. I saw the former as short, emaciated and over-earnest, the other as fat, sleek and very proud. I imagined one a worried junior English master at a Bombay secondary school, the other his bullying, vain headmaster.

For want of any other partner I went with Iris to a much-awaited jazz disco down in Whitehaven. She called for me dressed in a most ravishing outfit, scented, made-up, and alive and bristling with anticipation. We danced twice or thrice that night, but there were people there I recognised and managed to talk to for much of that lengthy evening. She had friends here also and it was a small enough affair for neither of us to feel uncomfortable about my independence, or could it have been, plain deviousness? It was such an innocent evening out that I asked her a second time, perhaps three weeks later, if she would care to attend the forthcoming party in a huge, old mansion not far from Maryport.

Again she was pleased and again we attended together, though this time with a seemingly more needful patience she followed me from room to room where a band, a disco, a string of comic films, and various other entertainments were in progress. It was an enormous party with at least half of West Cumbria's teachers, social workers, community workers etc. dancing, kissing, committing adultery, weeping, getting drunk or being sick. I was depressed by it and by Iris' desperate tagging beside me. She seemed to know almost no one here, the place and the number of partygoers were massive and daunting, the only relief she could gain was in sitting hard by me and doing everything short of holding to my arm.

Perhaps I overdid the kindly ignorance of her clenching, straining, waiting, hoping, and ultimately - in despair - sighing. As we sat on the couch among the hundred and twenty or so who were milling on that downstairs floor, it finally impinged on her that that protective distance of mine was obdurate and endless. Her chauffeuring me around, hanging on my heels and words, her presents of Indian titbits, her meal, and then the pathetically unrewarding bed and breakfast, were all as fruitless as the mazes and executions so apparent at this huge and monstrous party from which both our sensitive souls so painfully shrank.

She ferried me home this time at speed, at sixty, seventy, suicidal haste. Her face wore a look of tightly-bottled fury. I sat in undemonstrative silence, curiously unafraid of the ridiculous way she was driving. When she dropped me off she even bluntly refused my sheepishly polite offer of a cup of coffee. She revved up and whistled off with an aggressive, impudent goodbye.

Inside the house, solitary again, I strained to feel contrition where none would come. To be sure I had worries of my own at the time and I did not feel a great deal stronger in this lonely world than Iris did. I supposed, however, I had better stop giving her any hope at all of my meagre affections.

The next day I telephoned a woman I had been meaning to telephone for a long time. We arranged an evening out and later I and this youngish, wild and complicated girl, began a series of dates that led before long to at least one frustrated frustration. Curiously I mentioned nothing to Iris about this, though I reassured myself that it had nothing to do with her in any case. Now we studied Marathi together and that alone. I made no offers of evenings out at parties or discos or even attendance at a feeble lecture or a poetry reading. I thought I must be making myself plain, until Iris finally showed me how that really could be done.

It was on a Saturday when she came round apropos of nothing, simply for a chat and a cup of expensive tea. She had generously forgiven me my cruel self-protection and that serious, awful stoniness. As we sat and listened to some recorded Asian music she was lending me, she hewed her way slowly from that rock of nervousness and stated what was on her mercurial mind.

'We get on fairly well in certain ways,' she began, with unusual steadiness for her, 'but...'

She looked to me to help her out of that 'but'. I was tempted to let her stay hooked by her lips to her nemesis. Yet I had not the meanness, not quite enough, to watch the poor woman flailing.

'What?' I said gently.

'But... well, you know, how we've been seeing each other for Marathi... and for a meal, and the dance, and the party...'

'That party was awful wasn't it?' I stalled with a blush.

'And... well, you've been kind, and a friend, a good friend, almost like a brother... like a brother to me...'

I swallowed.

'A brother?' I said hollowly.

107

'Yes, and... well... I wish... I'd like... I'd like it if there was something a bit more... a bit closer... than just a brotherly regard... you held for me.'

Her courage in saying that prompted me into its like. I sought gingerly for the proper phrasing.

'Iris,' I said, wondering where I had heard all this before, if it was not in every dance hall and wise old American movie, 'I like you a lot. As a person. I do like you. But how can I put it? I don't... I don't really... I don't really *fancy* you...'

She gulped. 'No,' she said, as if in earnest disputation, as if conceding a just point. I listened sorrowfully to the echo of what I'd just said. I added quickly:

'What I mean... I mean... there are hundreds of people I don't fancy,' and I proceeded to enumerate mutual acquaintances whom I did not even remotely fancy.

'Oh yes, I see,' she said, trying to smile.

'Don't be hurt,' I said with a blush. 'There must be hundreds of men you don't desire either, but who you like to have as friends.'

'Yes.'

'I'm sorry.'

'It's all right,' she mumbled.

'Anyway,' I added softeningly, 'I am actually going out with a girl at the moment.'

'Are you?' she asked, not knowing whether to cheer or sadden.

'She's called Edna. She's a shop assistant from Maryport. We went to the same kids' school once upon a time.'

'Oh, I see.'

'I hope you're not hurt. I know how you feel perhaps. I was always wanting women who didn't want me. It's all relative. Isn't it, Iris?'

A few weeks later she gave up the Marathi, though that was subsequent to the time that Edna found herself another man for the next few evenings. I made no mention of this to Iris when she asked me kindly how my girlfriend was. She admitted that she wasn't getting very far with these Indian lessons and that in any case it was taking up too much of her time and money.

I lived in the cottage only another six months and in that time I had perhaps three more visits from her. She showed herself as neither condemning nor warm though she was in fact more friendly than hostile. It was on her last visit that a healthy-looking rage was apparent in her gestures and her words. Her voice had all the hoarseness of long suppressed anger, the same in effect as when she was drunk and ventured into quaky fields of irony, sarcasm and a simple playfulness. She was mad because it looked as if her despicable job was about to be prized from her.

'You know with these cuts in education they're contemplating...' she said, and then suddenly halted.

'Your job might go?' I suggested.

'Hah! The headmistress has hinted as much. Not on account of service of course, because I've been there for eight fucking years!'

It was the first time I'd ever heard Iris really swear. Her face was so red with passion it was like a blazing brand.

'Why?' I asked her.

'Why?' she echoed. 'Should I tell you why? Because the authorities that be, in education, will not promote me, but keep me at a junior semi-official status, and have done for years. And you know why that is, do you?'

I could guess, but pretended ignorance. 'Why? Tell me.'

'Because I've been in the bin all these times is why. Even though it's three years since anything happened. I was only in hospital then for four or five weeks. They'll never let me forget that blot on my credentials...'

I grunted. 'As if schools aren't the real madhouses. They're the last places entitled to get embarrassed about craziness.'

She wasn't listening, much less impressed by my antique observation.

'It's a conspiracy right enough. You break your back for these... swines... and do your duty... and smile, smile, smile,' she muttered.

After that it was ages, seemed years, before I met up with Iris again. I did though hear through a friend of hers that she had thrown in her job before they got round to giving her her cards. Rumour had it that she was in her house most of the time in Mula, painting, drawing and drinking as it took her. She was living on Unemployment Benefit, supplemented by a very few hours of some menial part-time work. I remember feeling glad for her and being happy to learn that she was enjoying herself at last.

I meanwhile moved closer to town and ended up living with a doctor's receptionist called Dinah Grey. Dinah was as it turned out a receptionist for a Workington doctor who had Iris on his panel, and so she was the first to tell me that Iris was back again in hospital for her nerves. I felt myself growing angry as I realised that obtuse cyclical model of hers had turned into accurate prophecy. She had caved in after another three years in the greater madhouse-at-large.

Some time later I was deliberating if and when I should go and visit her... when Dinah Grey informed me that Iris had escaped from hospital the night before! She had simply vanished without trace. All that was known was that her clothes were still locked in the hospital locker, so she must have fled in only a dressing-gown or in her skin. I didn't know whether to laugh or cry when I heard that last little detail. I had this picture of poor eye-staring, determined-this-time, desperate Iris, working her way through fields, roads, hedgerows on her way to God knew where. Perhaps to be raped, run over, murdered, and as if that hadn't been plentifully done to her in colourful ways already - was how my youthful rhetoric expressed itself.

At about one in the morning, just as Dinah and I were discussing the likeliest possibilities, an elderly and aggressive relation of hers appeared at the door. Apparently Iris had mentioned my name and whereabouts, in passing, at the paternal home and elsewhere. She seriously and not very tenderly inquired if I was hiding her niece. After that if I had any clue where the exasperating girl might have got to. Predominant in her demands were an elderly testiness, a feeling of family shame, and a largely trumped-up concern for her brother's daughter's welfare.

'You realise how much she could be a danger to herself? And do you know how she was discovered, the state she was in when we first had her committed last week? Have you heard the details, young man?'

'I haven't,' I said solemnly, still refusing to let her past the door.

'She was naked! Naked underneath a blanket and traipsing about with a whisky bottle.'

'In Mula?' I asked, refusing to be impressed.

'Lord no. If only it had been. It was in the Lake District... up in the fells near Loweswater...'

The year was 1975. It was June and it was scorching as of the last three weeks. The nudity seemed just enough, it was the use of the blankets that I couldn't fathom.

'You'll phone me if she comes here, or you hear anything more of her, will you?' she added.

'To be sure,' I nimbly lied, looking solemn once again as she scrutinised me insolently.

Naturally Iris was recaptured as of the next day, found barricaded inside her little terrace in Mula and yelling at the police who had her to go and do something to the real criminals in this world, those who had made it such a midden. They were very gentle, exasperatingly tender with her, she told me, on that day that I made my visit.

It was two days later that I went to see her, expecting to find her in bed, but instead there she was wandering anarchically around in a dull and ugly white dressing-gown. She talked officiously, bumptious and resentful, ignoring the tender queries and entreaties from the ever-cheerful gentry who make up the staff of a mental ward. They referred to her as *our* Iris, a stunning impossibility on every level and sub-level. One took it that if she was a good girl and didn't go jumping it again she would be recipient of more of this tender care, just as if she wasn't there would be the tender, gently chiding patience that would brush it aside as her illness and help her hospitably,

111

tenderly, pityingly to her carousel of pills, her helpful, tender electric treatment, a tender act of surgery being only a most remote and desperate possibility. The Indian consultant in charge wore that look of weary arrogance and petulance that he would also have had in Delhi, Madras or... Bombay.

She took me into the grounds surrounding - it was still a warm and sticky evening - talking at length and disconnectedly of all that she had been through. More than ever it was rage possessed her, fury at her impotence to be allowed to breathe.

'They needn't think that this bloody country is any different from what it was for Dostoievsky in Russia. They needn't look further for a police state than in here. They are bloody mad in here!'

I nodded. 'They look as if they kill you with kindness.'

'They treat you like children, those nurses. Like little kids. Whatever you say, however much sense, it's just your ravings!'

'There was this story of Chekov's...' I began to say, then seeing she wasn't interested in Russians any more... 'I heard from your relative about your trip round The Lakes, with only a blanket and a whisky bottle!'

She laughed with delight, with wicked hilarity. I looked at her and started to laugh alongside. We were like two lunatics together, two victims of a deep-seated sense of comedy.

'That was beautiful, that. It was. Until these charlatans came and put a stop to it. And my father and my aunts and whatnot getting the doctor to have me committed! I bet it was one he fiddles the tax for. Oh, but it was such paradise that journey. I was on a voyage. I've never had L.S.D. or anything like that but I know this was it. Everything was so beautiful, so pregnant with the divine! Divine's the one and only word for it. The lakes, the sun, the sky. Hah! It was like Blake. It was just like William Blake.'

I felt touched enough to look the other way. She stood up and started to pace about again. I followed her almost shyly as she roamed.

'I just took a blanket because it was so damn hot and yet I had to cover my body up. I had to get out of Mula because I was creating a scandal. Make no mistake! I was painting in the nude inside my house because it was so damn hot and the sweat was pouring from me. The whole village was coming to gaze. I just put my tongue out and waved. Then I got a phone call from my father's sister and she was furious. Someone must have told her what was going on. I could remember that terrible tone of voice from the last time. I knew I'd be committed so I decided to bugger off. I decided to fuck off and let them all stew in their... fear. I'm not afraid, look at me, I'm not afraid.'

'No,' I said sincerely.

'They're afraid. They're terrified. They are. Do you agree?'

'Yes.'

'We should expose them. You should expose them' - and then her eyes twinkled thoughtfully - 'You should have seen the paintings I was doing before they dragged me in here. They were so wild!'

She laughed with wildness also. I stared at her almost enviously. She returned my helpless stare quite playfully.

'One was of an old ghost, an old, old... God knows. He was also young. He was also a tree, seeding itself over and over and over. It was so damn hot when I was painting.'

I made a sympathetic noise.

'It might have been you. Yes, it had an element of you.'

'Me?' I said laughing.

'You could be a magician if you wanted. I used to think you were. You were so absolute and lonely.'

I blushed. 'I'm no magician. But at least I'm still lonely, Iris.'

'Eh? What about... Dinah is she called?'

'It's...'

'It's like a prison in here. They've taken away my clothes. They've drugged me up to the eyeballs. I have to fight against all this bloody leaden dope.'

I recalled all the other patients wandering around us before, as if all recently concussed. Tractable, pitiful, suffering without the noises.

'I'm going to fight it,' she declared eventually, 'as soon as I get out of this poxed-up jail.'

113

She was out after another two months. I saw her just as randomly and infrequently as before for the years that followed. About a year before I left the area and just as Dinah and I had parted, I met her down in Workington with a shopping bag full of vegetables. There we greeted each other with genuine tenderness, as genuine friends. And the first thing she did was to inquire after my girlfriend... what was her name... Dinah?

'We've parted,' I said, a little lugubriously.

'Really?' she asked in surprise. 'And I thought you were very strong together.'

She looked at me pityingly, gently, without any hint of rancour.

'What about you?' I asked eventually. 'I must say you look full of fire. You look as bright as they come.'

She laughed and flushed. 'I've got a job. Didn't you know? I have a job as a liaison person between the hospital and the new hostels, for the people who've just been its patients.'

'Really?' I echoed. 'I've never heard of a job like that. It sounds too sensible to be true.'

'Ach, it's only for a year,' she said wryly. 'One of these government schemes you know, to do something about the unemployment.'

'Oh yes,' I said vaguely, and then remembering something. 'And what happened about Bombay? Did you ever get a chance to speak Marathi to Prakash?'

She laughed again, full-blown and uninhibited. 'Marathi? That was a joke! Prakash hardly knew half a dozen words of it. All he knew was Hindi and a bit of Urdu. He was actually born in Uttar Pradesh you see...

Pleasure

To get to see Anna Fenster, Alexis Toner had to make his slow way down Pig Alley, always an anxious journey for one who disliked growling street dogs. He had to step through muddied ruts among the street's sulky inhabitants, the snuffling pigs. It was, Toner discovered, unnerving, the way in some Asian cities the progress from city centre to tip-suburb was accomplished in seconds rather than minutes. A dog followed him with mangy, suspicious eyes. Anna had said that a brandished stick would chase the dogs away. Toner halted and waited for rabid teeth to meet inside his leg, to contact raw bone. His teeth were on edge, his heart was racing wildly.

Anna Fenster lived in a tidy, rented villa, the rent being some few paltry dollars. She existed on her savings which had once been considerable and her present earnings which were rather variable. Anna had taught French Literature in a mid-west university for almost two years. Now at twenty-four she was retired; partly in order to write a wild American novel, wilder than any ever written was her intention. Her savings were supplemented by the posting of encapsuled hashish oil to America and the disguised importation of non-indigenous drugs to Nepal. Toner grimaced just at the thought of it. The peculiar ways of European and American travellers in this feudal kingdom of Hindus, Buddhists and ungenteel tourist. Witness The Pie Shop a few hundred yards past Anna's house where youthful travellers went to gorge themselves on five flavours of fruit tart, a speciality of Katmandu as well as English country tea houses. Witness The Pleasure Room, a cafe so called, where the customers sat on floor cushions around the perimeter of the room, guzzling bacon (yak meat) sandwiches, Cokes, chay, coffee, sugary cakes and most of them also sucking heartily at the frequent chillums of hashish being passed round the floor like a football tankard of ale. Tapes of British and American rock music augmented the pleasure of The Pleasure Room.

Anna went there frequently, as did her boy companion Dev. Toner wilfully avoided it, even if it meant leaving Anna Fenster for the evening and sitting alone in his hotel room.

Dev was a handsome sixteen-year-old and was apparently Anna's lodger. He was a Bhutani and claimed to have blood connections with a king of Bhutan. For reasons unintelligible to Toner he had been forced to leave that remote little kingdom. When not with Anna he gallivanted around the city with other young men, like any adventurous teenager. Toner gathered that he helped Anna in her commercial transactions and was rewarded with some sort of wage. That is, Anna kept Dev. Dev the Bhutani was always friendly with Toner but in other company he had seen him arrogant and spiteful. That delighted and entertained Anna who seemed to quietly enjoy intimate friendship with a penniless Asian and an Asian of one of the remotest kingdoms in the world at that. In fact Anna slept with Dev, something which Toner's sleeping self acknowledged but whose conscious self did not. He behaved like one in pursuit of a woman. Dev was kind to him, perhaps because he knew Toner would never get anywhere, not least because he was too old for her. For Anna liked teenagers, preferred adolescence to any other biographical state, unbeknownst to Toner.

Stumbling down Pig Alley he observed the unhinging handsomeness of the citizens, the great beauty of this mingled populace. In this borderland between China and India there was every variation of the Mongolian, the Indian, the hybrids. Those who partook of China and India, Toner liked to fancy, partook of both their ineffable ageless cultures, no amount of Occidental study of which would ever yield the faintest clue as to what it was to *be* a Hindu or a 'Sino-Tibetan' Buddhist. Some of the young men had eyes that were as large and tranquil as flower blossoms. They stared from a bedrock, looking at something Toner might never see, the shadow play of fluxing experience. They didn't fret, they didn't want, they didn't care, they didn't cogitate in any manner that he did. They dreamt, like aliens, like indifferent magicians. He had seen them up in the hills working on the roads. When a bus slowed down, the roadworkers would stare at the bus with that hypnotised self-sustenance, as if feeding off the core of tranquillity itself. And they were penniless, always poor, always a teeshirt and short trousers and that was all their trappings.

Anna Fenster met him at the door of her villa. Dev she informed him was out somewhere and Toner was pleased to hear it. Anna wore as usual her large black hat and her lively childlike smile.

'Tomorrow night,' she said brightly over coffee, 'they're holding a festival, a Buddhist one down Pig Alley. We'll go and see it, huh? It's a kind of masque, street theatre in fact of a heightened kind. There'll be blazing torches for illumination, some men dressed as devils and others as good deities. The devils will have the most terrible faces; enough to make you shit yourself and head for the hills.'

While speaking she took him into the sitting room and offered him some snacks. Then went on calmly to announce that *human* sacrifice was carried on in Nepal, certainly in parts of the remote countryside, but also in the capital here itself. Tantric rites connected with the goddess Kali-Durga demanding the blood of a young girl...

Toner frowned his disbelief. Anna laughed and her raw American laugh excited him.

'It's true, I'm telling you! Some little girl is secretly picked out by the initiates, the secret Tantric participants. They think of her as an incarnation of Kali and they watch her grow, keep their eye on her from a discreet distance. Of course she doesn't know, it's kept from her very carefully. Then, when she reaches puberty - I forget the precise age - her proud parents who have known about it all along, they take her along to the Tantric rite and sacrifice the little girl's blood to Kali!'

Alexis Toner froze. Something in Anna's tone seemed almost proud to relate such a grotesque anecdote, almost happy at the very thought of ritual bloodletting.

'I don't believe the parents would be pleased,' he said disgustedly. 'Who told you that, Anna?'

'Dev did once,' she grinned unabashed. 'But others, other

117

Nepalis. The police try and stop it but you know Nepali police are the dumbest in the world, specially chosen. Their wage is non-existent. What's more...'

'I don't believe it,' he interrupted determinedly.

'I don't see why not,' Anna replied indulgently, for she was after all two years his senior. 'You've come here via India haven't you? Young women set on fire with gasoline when their dowries aren't up to scratch. Untouchables, little kids included, having their eyes gouged out and their hands chopped off, a favourite way of showing them their place. This is bloody Asia, boy, not Canterbury nor Salt Lake City.'

Toner kept quiet. Those undeniable atrocities and the supposed compliance of parents in their childrens' bloodletting... those didn't excuse Anna's muted pleasure in relating such grotesque events.

'Anyway,' she added wryly, 'I can think of worse things than being sacrificed to a goddess. A standard middle-class American childhood for one. I recall being sacrificed to various gods and goddesses myself. I gather you didn't thrive on English Oxbridge and all the rest of it, neither?'

Which insinuation led eventually to a further exchange of biographies, her former university work, his future career, her present occupation of writing. Toner asked about her book and she explained that it was to be a bizarre comic fantasy about Nepal as experienced on hallucinatory drugs. As for Toner, who was enduring his present boring wait for money because of non-hallucinatory drugs, his nerves bridled at the apparent fearlessness of Anna's experiments. Her writing sounded fearless, her life itself seemed more bold and risky than anything he could stomach. Even so, he was perplexed that she should find it necessary to write about this exotic, peculiar country from an artificial psychedelic perspective. Did they not have the expression 'coals to Newcastle' in America he wondered silently.

'One of the sadhus at the Hindu temple, the big one, I give some free hash to whenever I see him,' she remarked as she expertly filled up a chillum.

'Oh?' he said nervously. After his recent insane exploit, he had no wish to touch any hashish for another five decades at least.

'Yep. We're buddies. One day I showed him some New York acid and asked him did he want to try it. He looked at me the way they do, inscrutable but kind. Weighing the consequences. O.K. he said. He goes away with a tab. I saw him two weeks later in the city. He came up to me and said. "Look, don't play with *that* stuff, Anna. It'll drive you crazy, Anna. It is bad, it is a bad bad thing." He tells me oh so seriously, like only a Hindu can.'

She laughed raucously at the memory, at the idea of her giving up L.S.D. Then she offered Toner from her chillum. His fingers trembled as he took it and elaborately pretended to inhale, while in fact only holding his breath and taking almost nothing.

Alexis Toner walked over to his hotel room's window and stared across at the closed courtyard, at the rear of two other hotels and of two large repositories of Tibetan merchandise. On the dusty earth that filled the yard pattered half a dozen filthy, dishevelled ducks. The constant courtyard music filling his room was the thud, thud, thump, thump of the miller's pounder, the big wooden mallet on a kind of rocker arrangement, the miller seated squat on the earth, heedless of the wandering ducks much less any world outside his yard. His wife moved about on errands difficult to categorise. Fetching this, looking at that, looking for something or other. Who knows, wonders Toner, if it is his wife, it might in fact be his daughter? But no, there is something about the way she moves past him and by him, a silent amity, the way of a wife who is calm and content in her marriage. For he has his own little business and they are evidently not starving. Just the ducks, rummaging forlornly in the dust...

A miller and his ducks outside and inside, in Toner's hotel room, three young men are scrutinising a political article in the *New Statesman*. It is about Vietnam (the year is 1973)

119

exceptionally well-written, densely idiomatic and highly intellectual English. And, to Toner's amazement, these young men understand it all, or appear to do so. Three young Nepalis, students at the Polytechnic here in Katmandu, are his pupils. He has gone over it with them verbally and now has set them some written comprehension. This is the first time Toner has ever taught English, or anything else for that matter. He teaches, perforce, because he is almost penniless.

One week ago, an endless aeon of his imagination, Toner got drunk on *Khukri* rum in *Hotel Britannia,* the only public house as such in Katmandu, run by Americans fittingly enough. As if that was not enough, he accepted a piece of hashish from a German who had just sailed through Kabul before the Afghan borders were to close, and was bragging about the quality of his purchase of Afghan black. As if that was not sufficient, Toner laughingly swallowed whole that biggish lump before staggering back to his hotel, the one he'd occupied prior to this one. Vaguely disquieted on his return, remembering the mechanics of swallowing as opposed to smoking powerful euphorics. That anything in the stomach must work its way out of the system in spontaneous autonomic manner, it is not like a joint which one can stub out or refuse if one has had enough. Once swallowed the child is yours, it and your blood are placentally intimate. The finger-end of ecstasy etc. is stuck there and will not be aborted.

About an hour later he was in a dreadful state, one which he bore in silence and in terror. Semi-naked, he lay flat on the bed, unable to do anything else. It was as if he was melting into a sand dune, all his viscera and blood system were turning into a scramble of desert and sable liquefaction. The sounds outside his room - the hotel check-in; the bawling of the boss to the servant boy; the occasional motor car passing - all sounded as if a thousand miles away, electronically remote. At one stage the servant boy came in to ask him something and Toner had to mumble that he was drunk, he had effortfully to make utterance. The boy grinned, Moner his name, six months down from the hills and still waiting for his first indentured payment. He was a rather pitiful broken-toothed teenager. Compared with Alexis Toner though, suffering a kind of hashish psychosis, he was in the pink in no small measure...

Then, after maybe half an hour of this passive immolation of his, Toner managed to rouse himself sufficiently to make it to the showers. He had the fuddled inspiration that cold spraying water might cool down his internal combustion. Off he stumbled to the douche where he locked himself in, hastily and carelessly threw off his underwear, and then stood underneath the spray. He also jumped up and down on the spot, like some deluded athlete, hoping that his bouncing would shift the lump of hashish and help it to speed its way out of his stomach.

Quite understandably he thought he might go mad, perhaps need the attentions of a hospital or a foreign doctor. He felt ashamed of himself, quite reasonably. He could see in advance the impatient looks of the Australian mission nurses, scarcely moved to the core by this tale of juvenile stupidity. Toner was twenty-two and ought to know better than to play the reckless sybarite. He was simply not up to it. It was too much for his naive capacities. 'The young fool drank too much one night, then swallowed too much Afghan dope, then went bloody haywire and we had to...'

What? He panicked at his cruel disintegration. Oh God, what a damn fool! He turned the water on further so that it began to splash to the sides and wet his underclothes. He swore. Such self-disgust was as fierce a torment as this inner incineration. Melting inside and chafing at himself simultaneously, he turned off the shower, rubbed and dried himself, put back on his underwear and towel and returned to his room. There he lay shaking and hating himself until unconsciousness overtook him and he fell into dreams of disrepair and incandescence, a displeasing medley of images of lonely bedsits in lonelier English university towns, Calcutta and its hideous, exciting streets, relations, friends, obscurities, and dead domestic pets. There was much of grief, an Arctic coolth of grief turned incongruously into red hot hashish dreams in that night before the morning after.

He awoke the next morning cold sober and immediately reached for his money. Into his underpants, the place where he always kept his moneybelt, repository of his English traveller's cheques. He fumbled. He kept on fumbling and - terrified - contacted nothing.

Hysterically he fumbled further, inside his jeans, and was deluded for a moment into thinking his belt must be in there. For he soon unearthed his passport and a wallet containing about forty pounds in Nepali rupees and sterling. Damn it - if that was there, so must be his traveller's cheques, the three hundred pounds of cheques! He must have the wherewithal to complete his stay here... even more important the money to leave Asia by plane at any time in the event of famine, homesickness, cholera, typhoid, hepatitis, jaundice, dysentery, the things which even the West could not buy itself free of, the things which hit the puny little body.

Nothing. No belt and no cheques. If he had calmly reflected, had he been at all equable, he ought to have been grateful he had at least his British passport. Instead, almost weeping, he dressed himself and ran to the shower to see if by more magic than that employed by the Creator at Creation his money belt was still there, where it must have dropped out of his underpants. The shower was occupied. He could hear a man singing in Hindi as he soaped. Singing when Toner was in such distress! Toner fumed and swore to himself, at himself, wanting to hit himself for his idiocy. Eventually the door opened and what looked like an Indian tourist emerged. He stared leerily at Toner. Toner ignored him, dived in, locked the door and commenced a pointless, over-extended search. Nothing! Not even body hair, nor condoms, nor a fifty paise piece. Not a sausage, not a Katmandu sausage, ha!

There followed a most distressing morning. He went first of all to the British Embassy where he had to wait a long time before being met by what seemed to be the owner of a yachting club, with membership tie to match. He was a diplomat. They gazed at each other with impolite distrust. The diplomat refused

122

at once to lend Toner any money and went on coolly about all the instances of fraud the Embassy had been put through by just such people as Toner. Toner's vehement denial of fraud, the sincerity of his anguish, scarcely seemed to pierce the diplomat's weary obstinacy. Instead, addressing Toner as old boy, he advised him to get along to the police to get a certificate of theft, then post that home to London, the place where the cheques were issued. There was unfortunately no Cook's office in Katmandu. Also to cable to any friends or relatives who might lend him some cash in the meantime. No by God, he added when Toner admitted he still had forty pounds in his possession, he would need to be in a lot worse pickle than he was at present to be getting handouts from the Embassy. In the meantime he might also... move into a cheaper hotel, obtain credit facilities from the manager and so forth?

Toner miserably left the Embassy by cycle rickshaw and returned immediately to his hotel. His behaviour then was most discreditable. He kicked up a fuss at the hotel desk and accused various of the staff of taking his cheques, for now that he thought about it there was a fair chance the money belt could have been lying in his unlocked room while he was having a shower. He remembered that he had been lying in only his underpants, on his bed, while fighting the drug poisoning, and it was... Moner... had looked in to ask him something or another. Moner, his little friend up to now, with set jaw he sought out Moner and demanded to know if he had seen or touched his traveller's cheques. Moner's patient incomprehension enraged Toner's scratched and stricken nerves. To have awoken from drug poisoning to financial destitution, then a snottish rebuff from the British Embassy, now nothing but the prospect of endless trips to police stations, telegram and post offices, banks and...

'Why was it you came into my room last night?' he interrogated the teenager, who ironically was wearing a dandy Pierre Cardin shirt that Toner had given him some days ago. 'What was it you came to ask me, Moner?'

'Because to tell you we had no Cokes,' replied the country

boy patiently.

'What?' snorted Toner. 'Why? What the hell for?'

'Before you went upstairs, you asked me to fetch you up a Coke. I couldn't find any, we were out of Coke. I came up tell you and you said you were drunk. You looked ill to me. I said do you want a lemonade and you said no, go away, you said you were drunk.'

Moner looked offended but not surprised that his friend should turn on him. The two managers of the hotel, men in their middle twenties, bawled and whined at him day in day out, as well as paying him no wages. Toner then beheld Moner's innocence, the obviousness of it, and felt quite shamed.

'I... look...' he went gently, 'do you recall seeing my cheques lying around in the room? Did you not see anything? Did you not?'

Moner shook his head.

'I'm sorry,' said Toner. 'I'm just very upset. I've got almost no money.'

And had Moner? Moner was not fooled. Europeans pulled money out of fresh air, like magicians. Their money was easy; cheques, signatures, banks, all the mysteries of the best Katmandu shops.

'I am sorry, Moner.'

Handsome faces. On those hundred steps at the end of the market, hundreds of small boys flying kites, their faces turned up to their hundred toys in all mature seriousness. This was the ancient, ineffably Chinese aspect of Nepal. The faces too of Tibetan refugees, scraggy little girls of compelling beauty, quite unworldly faces. Three of them regularly begged outside the dairy, the one place in Katmandu where one might purchase fresh milk. They begged without fear, as if demanding a right. They were willing of course to accept milk in lieu of money. They irritated and charmed Toner who was miserably waiting for his cheque refund from England. The Tibetans were the Jews of Nepal, cordially detested. They lived in the main in squalid refugee camps, in a country where the average wage was a dollar a week. The richest of them however ran the cafés and the trading posts in central Katmandu, for they had an enterprise and a flair for trade that exceeded that of most Nepalis.

Anna Fenster always gave rupees to the faces outside the dairy. They knew her and called to her like a sister. She knew some of them as pupils because for several hours a week she taught English in a Buddhist orphanage. She did this arduous work for nothing, this one who talked vauntingly of child sacrifice. And among other idiosyncracies she was enamoured of elaborate cosmological theorisings such as those of Velikovsky. She was also passionate about the tormented poetry of John Berryman. Toner who had a few books in his possession, gave her a copy of Berryman's poems, one he had purchased in Calcutta. He also bought her other books in the fine big bookshop near the Central Post Office. There they browsed together over the English paperbacks and the books from the Indian presses. Toner found himself leafing through *Outline Of The History Of The World.* It felt appropriate, such a work, in the shadow of the Himalayas. He saw a Colette novel and bought it for Anna. He bought her poems by Donne. He was cautiously spending his last forty pounds but spending without caution on Anna. She took his gifts rather awkwardly, the bright confidence was made a trifle stilted.

Anna was all face, her face was all of Anna. She was very beautiful to Toner's fraught, myopic eyes. He met her for the first time in Eat At Joe's, a Tibetan café that wisely served dishes from every country in the world for every possible tourist. Joe served pizzas, Canadian dishes, American apple pie, *chili con tacos,* Welsh rarebit, as well as Nepali, Chinese, Burmese and Indian cuisine. Joe worked on principles like the chapati principle. Pizza was chapati plus Joe's tomato filling. American apple pie was chapati with stewed apples in it. Pancake was unadorned chapati. It was a small low-ceilinged place with a cheery twelve-year-old waiter who wore a filthy vest and a bright red head band. There was an old patient man who sat at the door to take the bills as one left, perched up high like a parrot. Joe himself, the cook, was never seen. The air buzzed with English, French, German, Swedish conversations. The place was small and cramped and it was inevitable one would share a table. One day at his table appeared Anna Fenster with her pot of cream curd and her glass of fresh lemon juice. Toner who sat opposite was eating the same delicious combination. She asked him very deliberately was it no one else's place. He smiled an affirmative shyly. She seated herself nervously, as if she had made some kind of irretrievable gambit, and immediately brought out a notebook which she began to fill at reckless speed.

Her face was one he had seen many times, mostly in his childhood. She wore rimless glasses which gave her an angular, slightly Japanese, even a Chinese mien. Her hair was fair and thick and shiny to the point of edibility. Toner wished to bite her hair and *taste* it. Her cheeks were high-boned and also coloured crimson. She seemed to have patches of strawberry jam on each cheek. It was inviting enough for one to hope to spoon it from her cheeks. Her eyes blinked fast for she was nervous and reactive, a real American. Her voice was the deep scratchy New York voice. And that black flopped hat which she wore like a travesty of a snob at Ascot.

Their eyes caught. Both wished to make contact though Toner was to wonder eventually why. Did she feel a little feeble having only a teenage lover, a mere boy? Did part of her wish for an older man? Was Toner sufficiently meek and sad-looking to make the gamble a rather token one?

The London agency cabled him that he might alternatively travel to the nearest Cook's office on the sub continent and seek his repayment there. A thousand miles to Delhi which he had left only a week ago, was out of the question. Toner would instead bide here in Katmandu and wait for the reimbursement. He arranged for it to be dealt with by the Nepal Capital Bank, by what they told him was its head office in the capital. This involved all in all three or four expensive telegrams, air mail letters to London by the dozen, multiple rickshaw rides to the suburban head office, and a visit to the Central Police Station. It was all to-ing and fro-ing for day after day, like an exhausting dream or a frustrating search for some non-existent job.

At the police station he was introduced to the very young chief constable who kindly provided him with tea but throughout the transaction - Toner stood several yards distant - was trying on cheap jacket after cheap jacket after cheap jacket...

'Does this one suit me?' he asked Toner earnestly, as he tried on the tenth identical jacket, taking it from the patient hands of a servant who had another ten jackets in his arms. He looked in fact unimpressively clad, a sparrow in a meagre garment.

Whose jackets? Where did they come from? Why *so many* identical jackets? 'Oh yes,' Toner said generously. 'It's a very good fit.'

The chief constable was about twenty-one, tall and thin and improbably handsome. He soon provided Toner with his chit but insisted that he bide an hour or so to approve the rest of the mysterious jackets. He asked after the tailoring in London and so on.

This was not the only strange behaviour Toner encountered during that mammoth hellish wait for his reimbursement. He was to wonder why for instance there was such a delayed response to his English tuition advertisement in *The Rising Nepal* daily newspaper, for no one showed any interest until two weeks after it appeared, when three young students arrived all at once, at his hotel. Why had they waited those two weeks? On another occasion he visited a Professor Bajrachasya at the Polytechnic, a man whose name had been given to him by a vague yet playful academic friend in London. He turned up at the Professor's one room faculty to find the old man sitting in the middle of the completely furnitureless room, smiling stupidly while a hundred or so students wandered about him in all directions laughing and joking as if he and they were all being exercised in some closed mental institution. Perhaps he *had* come to a mental hospital by mistake? The Professor to Toner's embarrassment knew no English at all, but one of his students said that the faculty was 'undergoing extensive refurbishments...'

And he borrowed old magazines from the British Institute, and four copies of Gissing's *New Grub Street,* to help with his English lessons. He went to considerable pains yet found difficulty in extracting more than four rupees per hour from each of his students. The eldest and spokesman for them all, Krishna, claimed that it was all they could afford. Yet obese Krishna openly chainsmoked imported cigarettes which cost more than four rupees per pack. Anna Fenster later informed him that Krishna was the son of one of the wealthiest businessmen in Nepal. She had reason to discover as much if only because Toner eventually tired of this almost profitless teaching and went off to Pokhara for a time, leaving Anna with the tuition and the students. Krishna at once made efforts to seduce her and took her expensive presents, ones far in excess of four rupees. Toner and Krishna both employed the present-giving technique then, yet the Englishman quietly condemned it in the Nepali. He was jealous on all sides and particularly of the Bhutani Dev and Krishna the portly gift-bearer.

Hence Toner was making little progress in any significant direction. Twice a week he took a rickshaw down to the Capital Bank headquarters, a real milling hive of a place where most of Nepal seemed to invest its rupees. There he sought out the foreign transactions man who wore a clean white suit and a friendly face. There always there was nothing from England for him. Nothing. No foreign cheques for Mr Toner. What *were* they doing in London, he pointlessly grumbled to the man. Why were they taking so bloody long with his blasted money?

In the meantime he hired a large rickshaw to take Anna and himself to Bhadgaon, where they surveyed the lovely temple of King Bhupati Malla and he slyly surveyed lovely Anna Fenster. They talked about books, poetry, America and England, they spoke about everything but meaningful intimacy. She referred obscurely to men back in the United States who had pursued her for nothing but sex. She called them disdainfully fuckheads, on the analogy of potheads and acidheads. So that 'fuck' presumably was assimilated to the status of chemical in some corner of her reasoning, Toner realised. He told her about his future career when he returned to England, how he knew he ought to be grateful for it and to relish its prospect... and yet... part of him knew he didn't relish anything. He envied her for being a writer, a really bold occupation that one, one to bow down to as far as Toner was concerned. And yet he personally had no wish to read anything she'd written, because a psychedelic fiction set in Nepal simply failed to intrigue him from this distance. Only Anna's face itself inspired his excitement from this distance, at this precise moment.

They were just then seated in a dusty little café in Bhadgaon, eating hardboiled eggs and curds. It was here she told him raffishly of her commercial operations. At once he was entranced and equally irritated by her acquisitive face, one of her various faces. Her means of income part of him found despicable albeit in the abstract her daring, her very illegality, was impressive. He admired her anarchy yet denigrated the crass hedonism that was so much of this foreign contingent in Nepal and India. Writing an acid novel and dealing hashish in a country that was poverty-stricken, with a police force run by jacket connoisseurs, governed by a monarch who claimed to be the tenth incarnation of Vishnu, as well as an Oxford man. It was comedy and tragedy too heartlessly intermingled. It was like the journalism and the wireless programmes. *The Rising Nepal* daily paper - it had to be seen to be credited. The salty wisdom of the monarch took up eighty per cent of its extraordinary copy.

We must face obstacles and shoulder responsibilities and look to the future and take action where it is appropriate and not neglect our duties and above all... face obstacles and shoulder responsibilities and look to the...

Anna Fenster proved evasive about her precise past, discursive and jaunty only about certain neutral matters. Her family he discovered nothing of but he learnt that Anna was an identical twin and she believed that in itself had been deeply deleterious to her past and future. Also, just before leaving

America, she had shared a house with a married couple who had begun some peculiar exclusion tactic on Anna, ignoring her presence and trying to hurt her in needless petty ways, like some Oedipal fiends. It became apparent that she used her hashish and L.S.D. as intermittent boosters and modifiers like electronic apparatus designed to change input and output in a convenient repeatable manner. She intrigued and horrified him, attracted him and frightened him. The ignorant would have said that she was part of a placeless, rootless drug culture transposed several thousand miles, that the drug preceded the woman, the drug was the cause of this particular woman's poverty of language, poetry and expectations. But Toner from his own experience knew that if there had been no drugs involved there would still have been Anna Fenster, the same sort of woman. Her poverty might have been expressed as religion, fads, neurosis, it might have been anything, but one way or another it was Anna Fenster's will and heart, perhaps her soul, that had brought her to this bizarre role of transposing the worst of the West on to the poorest of the East as she wrote her psychedelic novel about Katmandu.

After many long days of teaching English and traipsing vainly to and from the bank, and a dozen frustrated efforts to decisively win the heart of Anna Fenster, Toner decided to try to provoke a significant change by setting off on a solitary vacation to Pokhara...

Without delay he purchased a bus ticket and sent a note round to Anna with details of the tuition he'd passed on to her...

The Sikh bus driver took it upon himself to fly at reckless speed around the thousand hill bends and virtual precipices. Toner, intrigued by the sights outside, forgot for a time his concern for money and for Anna. He beheld the countryside, the subtly terraced hillsides. He saw the roadworkers, teenage boys standing like dreaming calves, with their picks, their poverty and their unconcern. They wore the Nepali hats, plant-pot-shaped and worn by all the men, young and old. At one slow hill ascent he saw something that pierced him in a touching, obscure manner. A farm labourer was being washed by his wife in the open field, she was giving him a public bath. He stood in nothing but his loin cloth and his hat and at the rear she was rubbing his neck, back, thighs, backside and legs with a soaked cloth. His skin and muscles could be seen relaxing and healing themselves under the cleansing and the massage of his tending wife.

Toner wondered at that relationship. A man and his wife tending each other. Instead he saw strange Anna and saw his strange self. The bus halted and two little boys got on it with baskets of guavas, fresh ones that made Toner's mouth water. They were asking only one rupee for a huge basket and that was the inflated tourist price. This lunatic cheapness; Toner delighted in it and despised it. For his wealth was, of course, simply their changeless poverty. Weighed down under an ocean of guavas, he handed them round the whole bus and even then he still possessed a bucketful. Toner was sitting next to a Burmese who spoke very good English and the two of them were to overnight in a little village not far from Pokhara. The woman of the house killed a chicken as part of the price but Toner could not bring himself to eat it. It occurred to him that he had been neglecting his scrupulous hygiene regarding where and what he ate in these dysentery and hepatitis-rich regions... and he decided it was wiser not to eat the poor woman's chicken after all. She was of course openly hurt. The young Burmese was mystified. Toner found himself getting lost in an embarrassed explanation about stomach complaints and then opted in confusion to say that he had been very ill just recently. In any case, in the same place, there were two young peasants walking from Katmandu; by straps across their foreheads lugging huge baskets full of their master's produce. Toner anxiously urged them to eat his chicken. They were being paid scarcely a dollar to act the packhorse, two onerous miserable days on foot each way. The Englishman queasily could not bear the sight of such hardship. It made him all but hate himself. It made him want to empty his pockets and give these two patient paupers all he had. Even if he, in reality, was on his uppers, and many thousands of miles from his own home.

The Burmese and the Englishman slept in adjacent bunks that pitch dark night. While the Burmese talked about his policed and sealed-off land, Toner, as well as listening intently, stared at the fire flies dancing in the dense foliage outside their bedroom. He found himself suffused with the small poetry of childhood memory. Sparks flying, tiny incandescent magic, it was like Guy Fawkes Night 1956 when as a child he had watched the sparklers in the rough earth lonning in the back end of nowhere, an English hamlet little different in essence from the quiet Nepali hill village.

But his circumspection with the chicken unfortunately proved vain. The next day, in Pokhara itself, he entered an unclean roadside café where, being ravenous, he tucked into a large bowl of chicken curry. A few hours later, having explored the lake, the periphery of a Tibetan camp, and returned to his lakeside hotel to write some letters, he felt the first symptoms of something drastic down below. He went to the lavatory - a hole in the ground in a cubicle inside the rear yard - passed some faeces, and found them speckled with blood. There was also green fungus to behold, an unnerving proposition.

Dysentery! He had dysentery now on top of all his troubles! Already he felt as weak as a ghost and sensed himself just capable of retiring to his bedroom where he would collapse and stare in fetid weakness at the straw ceiling. The room was a sort of outhouse extension, raised up and approached by steps, its roof straw-thatched and teeming with many a creepy-crawly. Immobile on his bed the traveller would be able to do no more than stare at the insects crawling around in the straw. Luckily for him there were two single beds in the room. So when tired of one he could move despairingly to the other for a change of straw and of insect life.

In the spacious sitting room of Anna Fenster's villa sits an international circle, a unique symposium of its kind. Anna herself busily tokes the chillum like a satire on some anxious hostess mixing the cocktails for a set of her husband's business-friends.

Here also Krishna the chubby Polytechnic student with his expensive foreign cigarettes and his eyes never able to leave the magnetic brilliance of Anna. Dev the Bhutani, the little boy of sixteen, takes a dauntless pride of place, subtly disdaining all there except Anna Fenster and perhaps Mr Toner. Toner had arrived back from Pokhara over a week since yet he still has the remnants of his illness. Always thin, he now appears like a fleshy cadaver. He has been to the international hospital and had it confirmed that his dysentery is at least not the pernicious amoebic kind. A small comfort, pitifully slight. For his wretched money has still not arrived from London! It is now five weeks since he despatched the police chit to the travel agency in England. The delay is inexplicable unless quite simply Toner is cursed by a malevolent star. He disguises from present company that sorrowing hopelessness which came to him in its most virulent form in the thatched room in Pokhara where he lay enfevered, half-crazed. Now back in the capital, every time he believes himself recovered from the dysentery, he takes some nourishment, a boiled egg and some toast perhaps, and the gut infection starts up again almost immediately. Remorselessly. It seems therefore that he must either starve to death or have permanent dysentery - a condition peculiar to some of the remote hill people he has been told by omniscient Anna Fenster.

In the sitting room there is also a shy, dark-haired Canadian woman who has a strong sympathetic affiliation with Tibetan Buddhism. On account of which she has engaged the personal tuition of an old arthritic lama exiled from Lhasa. Lastly there is an older man, an ageing traveller who is all of twenty-eight or twenty-nine. He is Dutch, balding, unconfident and timidly ingratiating. Everyone except Dev feels bored by him and sorry for him. He has a strong theosophical outlook too, and is presently falteringly explaining some detail of Mahayana, some subtlety of epistemology. He uses the Tibetan terms he has patiently imbibed back there in Rotterdam. It is here, at precisely this point, that the heartless little Bhutani decides to rub the Dutchman's nose in it. Prince Dev happens to know some Tibetan himself and now aggressively mocks the pronunciation of the European. Moreover he pulls to pieces the Dutchman's hesitant explanation of the philosophical terms. It gets to the horrific, embarrassing stage where every sentence the stuttering bald man brings out is jumped on and cruelly demolished by Anna's messenger boy.

'No,' Dev scoffs in a boyish fearless way. 'That is pure rubbish, mister! It is *not* that. You have mixed up two terms that you shouldn't have and your pronunciation is just ugly gibberish. I am a Bhutani, mister, and I was taught my Tibetan as a child. I know as friends *all* the lamas in Katmandu here and I have read in the original many of the Mahayana texts that you are buggering up!'

Everyone except Anna squirms at such perverse brutality. Worse still is the reaction of the cowardly traveller who instead of slapping the little boy's ear for his insolence, as good as begs forgiveness from him. Toner is quietly enraged. Anna is quietly laughing to herself. A Dutch freak of thirty put in his place by a Bhutani prince just out of diapers what? The Dutchman grimaces cowardly complaisance, he has a face made wretched by confrontation. He backs down before the little boy like a terrified courtier. The boy smirks like some crazed turkey cock. Toner would like to wring his neck. And Krishna's too - that which is craned in exquisite over-attention to anyone and everyone in the room. But more especially to Miss Fenster. Krishna is terrified of missing a trick. Anna Fenster presides over all this comedy of manners with all the enjoyment of a wicked party hostess.

In Pokhara Toner's fever had raged. At night it was so much worse, in the darkness all alone Toner sweated and felt his thoughts race free like grinning dervishes.

First the memory of the Routing Of The Evil Spirits he had watched with Anna some evenings since, from the wall of her villa in Pig Alley. Rare 'street theatre' that had been. Terrible demons with grins of murder and thoughts of vicious rapine. They had teeth to rip out vitals, eyes to pierce marrows, jaws to crack bones, colours to instigate both a fear of light and fear of darkness. They made him fear for his choroid pigments. They had eyes gone mad with lust for murder and destruction. They drank the blood of babes, they chewed and swallowed genitals of innocents in a frenzy of depraved idiocy. They had power from the very root of evil itself, the lone self-feeding spirit of evil.

'*Get thee behind me,*' whimpered Toner crazily to one of the faces. '*I will not hear thee, demon!*'

It was monsooning outside. Rain rammed the thatch with brilliant violence. The febrile ears of Toner started to hallucinate music where none existed. All sorts of music. There was - listen! - some Mozart oratorio. He could hear it flinging itself across the silent lake and the towering Himalayas. Fat bellowing ladies and stocky, expressionless gentlemen in choruses sung in München and Würtemmberg.

'*Kyrie eleison, eleison, eleison...*'

'Hah!' laughed Toner at the image. Fat ladies hallooing and gollaring. Fat gentlemen roaring and declaiming. What mirth! What hellish splendour!

Dimly he saw a million ants a-crawl. He lit a candle to observe the ants in the thatch. He knew himself to be fevered and hallucinating alone in a hotel in the lap of the Himalayas, the home of the Hindu gods. Terrified, he went down the steps to the toilet, shivering in the pissing rain, and had to traverse the growling mongrel belonging to the hotel. He squatted over the hole in the cubicle and shat. There was some sort of ugly green insect, a large disgusting thing bobbing up and down like a soup ladle inverted in the hole. Toner shat on it. The dog growled outside. Toner cleaned himself and stepped past the dog, expecting it to tear off his legs. It growled again. Toner belted up the steps in terror, back to his bed and his visions and his ferocious exorcisms.

'*Get thee behind me!*' he roared in his fever to the thatch and the scurrying ants. He was afraid they would drop down onto him and he would swallow them up and catch some fresh disease. '*Get thee behind me, filthy demon!*'

Beside his bed lay the two books he had been trying to read during the less fevered daylight. *Headlong Hall with Nightmare Abbey* by Thomas Love Peacock; *Man's Estate* by Malraux. Thomas Love Peacock? Of all the possibilities, T.L. Peacock, read within spitting distance of the Tibetan border, the last estate of the imagination. Thomas Love Peacock in the land of kings, bandits, forbidden bandit provinces like Mustang. In the land of exportable hashish oil, of lone Occidental neurotics swallowing Mahayana and hashish from identical concentrated capsules. T.L. Peacock! Toner laughed so violently he thought that he would burst a blood vessel and have done with it. But, what, he asked the ants, didn't they have peacocks in the sub-continent, the indispensable of all their ancient love poetry? Weren't all the irreconcilables not so in these fairy countries, mountain principalities of Nepal, Bhutan and Sikkim, the furthest outposts of the lost British empire? *Eat At Joe's, The Pleasure Room, The Rising Nepal Facing Obstacles, Anna Gives Acid To The Sadhus, The Sadhus Beg To Defer. English At Moderate Prices From Mr Toner, Mr Electric Toner, B.A. Oxon (England, Europe). Saugata Toner Puts His Shoulder To The Cosmic Wheel Exerting All Spiritual Strength To Recover...*

He was talking his lustreless gibberish to Satan, the Anglo-Indian one. He thought he was going mad - all the way on wings. Yet, if he had attained to madness, he would never have known; it would have subsumed him like the Buddha all denials; Brahma all empirical reality; Jesus all self-deceiving lies. It would have taken him under its wing in its solicitous way.

While Anna Fenster taught penniless Tibetan orphans and in the evenings Krishna and his wealthy friends, Toner dragged himself from bed to bank, and back again to his Katmandu sickbed. His dysentery would not be cured, neither would his money arrive from London. His fragile invalid imagination aside, Toner was growing highly suspicious of the clerk at the bank. Communication between Nepal and London was slow, expensive and inadequate and yet the agency in London emphatically claimed by telegram they had despatched his

136

money three weeks since. Yet the foreign transactions man at the Katmandu bank swore that no such English cheque had arrived. Toner was just at the crucial stage of disbelieving a mysterious delay in the post and putting it down to... corruption, some crude fraud by the little Nepali bank clerk.

Corruption, baksheesh, to be sure it was a way of life in the impoverished East. It was frequently the only way for underpaid officials to survive. But with the money of *foreigners*, an international transaction like his? Toner kept asking himself over and over again, sleepless and quite witless with his dysentery.

Toner felt fully persecuted by his body which refused to heal, his money which refused to arrive, and by Anna Fenster who refused to be anything but wary. Yet she, he *knew* it, had sought him out in Eat At Joe's! She had made a very definite approach five weeks ago, in search of something she had wanted from someone like lonely young Toner.

His existence grew utterly unbearable. It got to the stage where he could not sleep a wink. He had had dysentery for two and a half weeks and always if he broke his fast the symptoms would return with fresh vigour. Insomnia and physical attrition made him panic, his nerves became overactive and exhausted. It occurred to him that if this kept on much longer he might well die or have some sort of breakdown. That made him swallow and panic even more, with a great self-pity. Money, women, illness, he forgot which was which, which came first, whether there was anything to distinguish the three unassailables. He came to the unoriginal conclusion in his lonely bed that a man who could do without a wife, without a job and without a body... would be a happy ghost.

He tottered onto the streets and sought out a chemist's for some sleeping tablets. In the East one buys one's somnifacients over the counter, like cough sweets. He purchased Mandrax to make him sleep. He felt like a junkie, it was disgusting, it was pitiful. He took one of his Mandrax that night, along with a glass of lemonade. It made no difference. He could not sleep. Instead he wove backwards and forwards between lavatory and bed, shiting blood and mucus and spitting disgust and horror as the days and nights went by like some jumbled horrible dream.

One early evening, just as the sun was waning, it appeared to Toner that his heart had stopped. He simply could not breathe. He panicked and felt his pulse. No pulse! He panicked and felt his heart. No heart!

Toner cried out. The cry was lost and inaudible for he was stone dead right enough. The miller was pounding and battering away outside, muffling everything save the faint quack of the ducks, sounds reminiscent of cinema animation. The ludicrous fantasy name *Devadip Duck* came into his mind. Yes, he was really dying, his system had stopped at last in protest at this never ending dysentery...

Dying? Toner who had more than once in his twenty-two years, dreamt narcissistically of a much admired death, suddenly felt a great urge to live. It came to him in an instant that he wished more than anything to live and keep on living for a very long time...

Still, he was wrapped around in panic, panic was his present element. He leapt out of bed and shook himself into life. He reached for pulse and heart again and detected a feeble stir. Life! Yes, yes, there was life in the old cadaver yet! He slipped on a few clothes and put his head out of the door. He saw one of the servant boys outside and implored him desperately to come inside. With great earnestness and anxiety he begged the boy to go and fetch Miss Anna Fenster, the American with the glasses. The boy's English was of course not very capable. Toner was wild with frustration. How to communicate such urgency? He sought a pencil and a piece of paper. He drew a map of Pig Alley and pointed to the house and told the boy he would give him *five* rupees if he would fetch Anna Fenster to his room. He gave him a scribbled message to give to the American lady with the glasses. He even did a rather peculiar drawing of Anna Fenster to assure the boy it was the American lady and not a little pig that he wanted from Pig Alley.

The boy departed with all speed. Toner staggered back to his bed. Then he counted the minutes until Anna came. He

138

expected to wait a good twenty minutes at least. Instead, in less than one, there was a knock at the door and when Toner shouted come in, Anna herself appeared with an unexpectant grin.

'Hi there,' said she, bland and blind to his miseries.

'It's you!' he whispered. 'Did you see him, the boy?'

She looked blank. 'Who?'

Anna had seen no messenger boy. Her arrival was a sheer coincidence, for she had just happened to be passing on her way to the Pleasure Room to see Dev.

From his bed Toner pitifully and hesitantly explained that he was... dying. True enough his eyes were burnt black with insomnia and panic. Anna Fenster loudly laughed. Toner almost cried. Alexis Toner however was not so far gone that he couldn't laugh a little weepily himself. He managed a feebly strangled chuckle.

'God, you look like a genuine cadaver,' she said cheerfully. She pronounced the noun to rhyme with shaver.

Toner feebly enunciated the summation of his troubles; the fact that his money still hadn't arrived; that his dysentery was just as bad, and worse than all of that, *he had not slept for days*. His sleeplessness was starting to get to his nerves, could she not - he tried to ask by telepathy - understand? He honestly felt as if he was going to pieces, his nerves felt so utterly weak and battered.

'Meaning you're bumming out I guess,' précised Anna Fenster calmly with an expert's diagnostic voice.

Was that all, sighed Toner to himself. Oh yes - she had the words for it. It was the same way she discussed types of chillum, acid, human sacrifice and so on, the words of the freaks. Didn't she see, cried Toner soundlessly, he wanted comfort, some kind of *recognition* of his bruises? As a young woman she should comfort a young man, she should play the wife if only for an hour or so. She should play the wife to a cadaver, a dying man! Toner was dying, whether Anna credited it or not - the least she could do was to proffer some comfort for his mortal, etiolated soul.

139

Anna Fenster was more than wary. She stood tensely in her rallying attitude, more hesitant than ever. She knew well enough what it was to be at desperation point, for what else had driven her to come all this way to live this particular life but a private desperation too cruel to disclose?

'Stay with me,' he begged her, sitting up in bed to make his grovelling demand.

'What!' she blurted, her eyes blinking at a furious rate. He saw her almost tremble.

'Stay with me tonight, Anna!'

She swallowed.

'I'll go crazy otherwise,' he insisted with wild, yet vacant eyes. 'I know I will! I can't sleep and I'm ill and I've nearly no money! I'm desperate! I feel completely desperate and exposed! I need someone to stay here and give me some crumb of comfort, Anna!'

It was his testament, the testament of Toner. He had almost choked with embarrassment to say it. He had bared his soul. He had obliged her to be honest now, having flatly stated his condition, his woes and his simplest needs.

'Look... look, look, I know what'll cure you,' she sidestepped with a vast flush.

Alexis Toner felt to the core her coarse refusal. She had denied him. Without ornament she had said, no! He was *alone* therefore, alone completely, in a nightmare sickbed almost as remote as fabled China.

'Opium,' she added in a quaky voice.

'What?' he said, trembling.

'The Nepalis use it to stop dysentery. It freezes up the gut muscle,' Anna explained, her discursive, instructive voice gradually finding its own confidence again. 'It's all they can afford, they haven't the money for antibiotics and hospital drugs. Take a little tincture of opium is my advice. It'll help you sleep for one, and for two it'll stop your bloody dysentery.'

Oh and as luck would have it, she had some in her bag, some she had been dosing one of the little orphans with earlier today. Some of those kids had near-permanent dysentery she calmly explained. For some of them continuous serious illness was just one of the trademarks of being a refugee orphan.

Toner felt ashamed of himself. For opening his heart. For being a Westerner. For being ill. For complaining. He remembered penniless Moner of the previous hotel. He felt like a spoiled baby and he felt repugnant. Limply he took Anna's bottle, then a minute sip of the opium. He looked at her. Would she laugh if she'd poisoned him by mistake? Didn't she laugh when she talked about human sacrifice? But what odds? He begged her again to stay with him, until at least he had fallen asleep. Anna blinked and grunted what might have been a yes. She coughed then said she was slipping out to get some orange juice, and she'd be back within minutes. She vanished like a dying spark. After the door had closed the servant boy came in with his worried young face to tell him the lady had not been there in Pig Alley. Toner explained what had happened and gave him the five rupees anyway. He waited for Anna to return and help him in his fight against the nightmare. He waited an hour but there was no return. She'd deserted him without a second thought. The opium - it had made him hollow, drowsy, reft of any feeling.

Then he fell fast asleep. Anna Fenster of course did not return. She went hurriedly to The Pleasure Room where she met Dev and a young Nepali businessman with contacts in the capsule business. She forgot Alexis Toner, blinked out of mind certain doubts and hesitations, as she forced herself to feel her great enthusiasms.

Morning. Toner, to his astonishment, felt a great deal better. The thought that dimly struck him on waking was that Anna Fenster had not come back to stay by his bedside. It was eleven o'clock and sun shone brightly on his table. The ducks and the pounding miller seemed to be rejoicing in the fine new day. Obscure and shameful fuddling of mate and mother occurred to him as he thought of how he'd asked her to be a nurse and mother for one night. He felt embarrassed, most puny in the world's eyes. Nonetheless, he was forced to console himself. If someone, if anyone had begged him in all sincerity for something so simple, he, Toner, would not have spurned them. He despised that undeniable personal cowardice in Anna Fenster, he briskly decided that her courage and recklessness were only relative and selective.

And yet... yet... at least her opium remedy had *worked*, it seemed to him. His belly felt better than ever it had felt. He felt almost *cured* of his dysentery. In the stinking lavatory young Toner observed his excrement to be stouter and healthier stuff than he'd have dared to hope last night.

That morning he was almost inspired. He hailed a rickshaw and afterwards created a disgraceful scene at the head office at the suburban bank. He accused the bank clerk of wilful deceit and threatened him with the attentions of the local police. The money had been despatched from London weeks and weeks ago, so how come this Capital bank could not hand it over, interrogated Toner. Eventually - the poor little clerk was petrified into making two or three white-faced phone calls to various other persons.

And eventually...

'Your money *has* arrived,' the little man mumbled glassily, the sweat just visible on his round, smooth brow.

'You have it?' asked Toner incredulously.

'Yes ,' the little man replied guiltily. Then stuttered. 'Not here though. It's at our *Head* Office.'

'*You... !*' gasped Toner, half-demented. 'But *this* is the Head Office! You yourself told me it was. You've told me so over and over again! For week after bloody week!'

'No, no!' choked the mortified bureaucrat. 'It is at our *Head Head Office*. This is only the Head Office! Our Head Head Office is up at...'

Hastily and with face down, he communicated the H.H.O.'s address. Toner was so pleased to hear his money was somewhere in Katmandu that he swore very meagrely indeed at the idiot of a clerk, this stupefying little man who had forced him to wait all these weeks for nothing. The money had arrived at the Head Head Office twenty-one days ago! Prior to dysentery. Prior to knowing Anna Fenster more than a few days! Anterior to much needless misery, eh? This little man's idiosyncratic stupidity had led hopeless Toner into two or three adventures far better not advented.

'Christ!' Toner swore, as his rickshaw took him the two miles to the Head Head Office. 'Christ!' he repeated loudly in a mystical excess of dumbfoundedness.

At the H.H.O. they wished to pay him his money in Nepali rupees instead of pounds-cheques. Toner gleefully banged his fist and said no, not Nepali rupees, which would have had to be changed into Indian rupees subsequently. Toner wouldn't even be satisfied with sterling in fact. Toner demanded U.S. dollar travel cheques, ones which had connections with branch offices throughout the remotest parts of the East. Never again would he risk having to wait for money from London. He would play the American if he could play nothing else! He would bank with America if he could not bank on that American Anna Fenster!

Yet when the time came, he managed a friendly goodbye to her. Three days after, rolling in dollars and rupees at last, he took her for dinner to an Indian restaurant, one of the very best in Katmandu. He even stole a kiss from her at the end of the day, the eve of his departure. They even sat late at night on top of the roof of his hotel and gazed at the sheet of blazing sunset, the vivid blanket of orange that looked like pure elemental ecstasy. She joked in the warm scented air about Dev the Bhutani who had been grabbed by the police, suspected of stealing temple idols for export to the acquisitive West.

'They were Coke cans!' she said hysterically. 'The cops saw him and his friends with two empty cans of Coke and decided they looked like stolen temple idols. So they took him to the police station and beat him on his feet. Then they beat him harder than ever when they saw they *really* were Coke cans and he was wasting their bloody time.'

At what would she not laugh, this doughty authoress? When he stole the kiss she looked amazed and more than a little feckless. She looked like a startled child. Toner laughed in a superior manner. They were almost equal. He told her determinedly she was beautiful, that he sincerely admired her, as she vanished at last into the darkness of stinking Pig Alley.